TOBY

A Novella

By

Thomas Watson

Other Books by This Author:

Nonfiction:
Mr. Olcott's Skies
Tales of a Three-legged Newt

The Process: Nine Essays on the Experience of Writing Fiction

Short Fiction (Science Fiction & Fantasy)
Chance Encounters
179 Degrees From Now

Science Fiction
The Luck of Han'anga
Founders' Effect
The Plight of the Eli'ahtna
The Courage to Accept
Setha'im Prosh

All That Bedevils Us: A Tale of the Second Iteration

The Gryphon Stone

CONTENTS

ACKNOWLEDGMENTS

With thanks to my wife Linda for once again insuring all my hyphens are in order, and for keeping my sentences straight. And special thanks to Ron Boe for making sure I hadn't forgotten anything important about dogs. If I missed the mark somewhere after he reviewed the story, that's surely on me.

To the dogs of childhood memory, Topsy, King, and Clementine.

« 1 »

The story happened, and then the story was told, and the telling became a story of its own. Or a part of the same story. Both are true, when you think about it.

*

The way they look at you when you walk by, it's a wonder any of them are ever in need of a home. The pleading eyes, the energy quivering in them as they sort of lean toward you as if trying to make a connection. The tentative tail wag that speeds up if you make eye contact, and slows as you turn away. Most people don't see what comes after that — the slow and subtle deflation into sadness, the eyes searching whatever foot traffic is passing by, looking for someone. Anyone.

I was resistant to that look most of my life. Oh, I saw it often enough, but it never moved me to take action. For too many years life was not conducive to the raising of pets of any kind, unless you count fish in an aquarium. Which I don't. That's more like having an animated stamp collection. It's a fine hobby and I enjoy it. It's the reason I was in the pet store that night, the evening I discovered that my resistance was gone, washed away by a pair of big brown canine eyes the year before.

The battered wire kennel with the dog in it was set up at the front of the pet store, pushed up against a second, smaller cage perched on a wooden box. In that smaller kennel a large black-and-white cat licked its paw. Both cages held water and food bowls, and folded towels meant to provide comfortable spots for napping. The towels had seen better days. The cat and dog were the only two animals present, the other cages being folded and stacked out of the way.

This dog bore a strong resemblance to the one I'd come to know the year before, the same build and overall coloring, a resemblance so strong that I did a double take and, in that moment, made eye contact. Pleading brown eyes, a stance that suggested some sort of psychic energy beamed my way and, of course, the tail wag. Ears and tail were undocked, so as a friend of mine would put it, he was someone's puppy, once upon a time, and not a dog someone felt compelled to alter for the sake of imposing an artificial standard of appearance.

This dog even had a blaze of white on his face, running up his muzzle, almost the same size and shape as the one on my recent canine companion.

The close resemblance took me completely by surprise; I was so distracted that I almost tripped over my own two feet. Even so, I was still about to walk on and finish my errand, so I could go home and wonder what to do with myself for the rest of the evening. I might even have had second thoughts about walking away from that dog. But the woman at the long, battered, wooden table spoke, and two heartbeats later the chance to simply go about my business was beyond recall.

"Are you all right?" she asked, looking and sounding concerned. "Pardon my saying so, but you look like you've just seen a ghost."

"Not quite," I replied, gathering my briefly scattered wits about me as I looked from the hopeful dog to the lone volunteer from the pet adoption group. I think pretty fast on my feet, most days, and outgrew my tendency to get tongue-tied in the presence of an attractive woman decades ago. "He..." I paused and took a quick look. Yes, definitely male. "He reminds me of an old friend." And felt a fond smile steal over my face as I said so.

"Ah," and she looked up from where she sat, two more brown eyes, these human and set in a face full of sympathy and understanding. "How long ago did he pass over the bridge?"

"The — what? Bridge?" I'd never heard the phrase before then.

"Um, how long ago did you lose him?" she asked carefully.

"Coming up on a year — oh, wait, I see. No, he didn't die. I just took him home." The quizzical look on her face prompted clarification, not that I felt any reluctance to talk to her. "He's back with his family, now. Where he belongs. With the people who love him."

"With all but one, it would seem," she observed.

I laughed at that, and she smiled at me, one of those smiles that transforms an attractive face into one of surprising beauty. Dog or no dog, I was in no hurry to move along with my errand. "Oh, he has no shortage of fans," I replied. "Though some of us who love the big dude are fortunate enough to have known that affection first hand."

The quizzical look deepened into a puzzled frown that all but erased the smile. "Do I know you from somewhere?" she asked. "I mean, have we met before?"

"No, I'd surely remember you if we had." And couldn't believe I'd said that. "I'm sorry. That was pretty lame."

The smile returned completely. "I will take that as a compliment, sir. It's cool."

"No, wait," I said as I suddenly recognized her. "Aren't we neighbors? Pretty sure I've passed you on my morning run."

"I think you're right," she said, smiling and nodding. There was a touch of mischief in her eyes. "Except that I'm the one passing you."

I feigned outrage for a moment, and we both laughed. "Yes, well, I only started running again a couple of months ago," I told her. "Used to run in 10Ks. I get back into that condition, and we'll see."

"I did my first half marathon three weeks ago." She chuckled as I sighed and let my shoulders slump as if in defeat. Tipping her head to one side, she seemed to consider something. "The morning run isn't the only thing, though. I feel like I'm trying to connect you to something else."

"Well, I've noticed you walking your dog in the evening," I said. "In fact, it's this big fellow here, unless I'm mistaken."

"I've been fostering him, and that cat, for about a month," she admitted.

"Hard to place?"

"His false reputation precedes him," she said, looking annoyed.

"I thought rescued pit bulls and pittie mixes were a thing, these days?" I asked.

"It comes and goes," she replied with a shrug. "Do you do something online? A weblog or podcast?"

I knew immediately what she was searching for. "Ever hear of a dog named Toby?" I asked. "He was something of a celebrity last year."

"That's it! That's why you look so familiar." The smile became a delighted grin. "I found the weblog his family set up when he was lost in New Mexico, and then followed along while you were taking him back to Illinois."

"You were part of an enormous crowd, then." It was, for a brief time, one of the hottest trends on the internet.

"It's still up, you know," she told me. "Your face is part of the cover page."

"Ah yes, the parting shot," and I chuckled as I spoke. "Not the best picture ever taken of me, but then, I was in a bit of distress. I didn't know Sarah took that until she asked permission to post it. Took it just before I left. And poor Toby, he really didn't understand why I was leaving. They told me later he stood at the end of the driveway until he couldn't see my SUV anymore."

"That must not have been easy," she said. "Driving away like that after all the two of you went through."

"It was and it wasn't. I missed him immediately." And if that wasn't an understatement. "But he was where he belonged. I mean, the faces of that family when he jumped out to run to them at the end of the trip. Those kids..."

"I can only imagine." From the shine in her eyes just then, it was clear she was not someone who routinely repressed emotions.

"Well, if you followed the blog, you have a pretty good idea."

"They did a good job, but it was mostly a second-hand telling of the tale." She shrugged again. "I can't help the feeling that a lot of detail was left out."

"That almost sounded like an invitation."

"Almost?" She laughed a little and glanced

at her watch. "I'm obliged to be here until they close the store at eight this evening. Down to this big fellow and his little neighbor, and this place is dead quiet." She suddenly looked so sad. "We're not going anywhere."

That was true enough. The only other person in sight was a cashier who seemed to have gone brain dead due to boredom. She just stood there watching us, though it was clear from her blank look that her mind was elsewhere. I was familiar with this pet store and had known they hosted pet adoptions in the past. They set up those adoption events so you can't go far into the store without passing the cages. From the empty kennel cages and pens stacked around the table, I guessed this one had been pretty successful. Only the big dog and the black-and-white cat remained. There was no figuring the cat, it was a pretty enough animal, but the dog being left over didn't surprise me at all. If he wasn't pure pit bull, there was enough of the breed showing in him as no matter. Not everyone is willing to take one on, given the breed's reputation.

"I'm certainly in no hurry tonight," I replied. Okay, I was looking for an excuse. She had, indeed, caught my eye on those morning runs, passing me like a bounding gazelle. Now that we were actually talking, there was a definite attraction, which seemed as mutual as it was spontaneous. There was something about her that went beyond the fact that I found her physically attractive, a forthright attitude that came from a certain degree of maturity. Neither of us were kids, and both had lines at the corners of the eyes and just a touch of gray in the hair — long and brown in my case, short and black and tightly curled in hers. She wore her years well, better than I did. No, not kids anymore, but not so close to middle age that we could feel it in our bones. Or so I assumed, in her case.

The dog kept his big brown eyes locked on me.

"And I am bored out of my skull," she admitted. "I'd appreciate the company and the chance to get to know a neighbor. I haven't lived there long, and don't really know anyone. It would be nice to change that, and I would love to hear the whole story first hand." And in haste added, "I mean, if you don't mind?"

"I don't mind at all," I said, pulling out the only other chair at the table, and sitting facing her with the dog on my left.

"I'm Samantha," she said, holding her hand out across the table. "But my friends call me Sam."

The dog made a whine that sounded hopeful as I shook Sam's hand. Her grip was warm and firm. "Hey, easy does it, buddy," I said. "Haven't forgotten about you." I put my hand to the side of the cage and a big, wet nose pushed at it through the mesh. "I'm Paul," I told her. "But you probably know that already."

"Paul Ford, yes, founder and former owner of Celestial Graphics and Effects," she said with a nod. "Your young friend in Illinois, the one managing that weblog, gave you a plug in about

8

half the entries."

"She's hoping for a job, and if she comes to school out here, I will see to it she has one. And as it happens, I'm back in with the company now. I sold it to my employees and they took it to the next level, and then some." I shifted my weight in the chair, trying to settle in. It was not the most comfortable folding chair I'd ever encountered. "When my trip with Toby was over, they asked me to come back in. So now I'm just another employee owner."

"That must be kind of odd, going from numero uno to just one of the crew."

I shrugged and said, "Not really. The guys and gals calling the shots are better at it than I was. Now I'm focused entirely on the creative side of things, leaving the business aspects to those with a stronger entrepreneurial bent. Having the time of my life." I wasn't blowing smoke, either. Life, in that regard, had definitely been on an ascending curve since my trip.

"You're a lucky man, Paul." She looked sort of wistful. "Most of us have to find something like fulfillment outside the regular job."

"Don't I know it. Been there, done that. Then I took a chance to strike out on my own and got really lucky!"

"Luck is no stranger to you, it seems," Sam said.

"Not always the case," I admitted. "But it certainly followed me closely last year."

"Not just you."

She might have meant the dog named

Toby, but I had a feeling she was thinking of someone else. I was for a moment a little uncomfortable. "No, not hardly. But that's getting ahead of things. A well-told tale starts at the beginning..."

« 2 »

It may well be true, what I said about a well-told tale, although beginnings often seem arbitrary.

So, start this one with me in a campground somewhere in northern New Mexico, a few miles from a small town that doesn't show up on most maps. I'd gotten there in a roundabout way from San Francisco, hitting the road shortly after the end of my marriage and the sale of my share of interest in the company to a bunch of eager youngsters. Money was no longer an issue for me, and likely wouldn't be for years to come, the court having shown my ex no mercy whatsoever. That she was about to serve some pretty heavy time for money laundering certainly didn't hurt my case. The FBI had come to me saying they believed someone was running drug money through my company. They were already convinced — never told me how or why — that I was innocent of wrongdoing. But no one knew the inner workings of CGE better than I did, and they needed my help on the inside. I almost swallowed my tongue when they laid that on me, it was such a shock. And then I was more than willing to assist them, and also seriously pissed that it was happening. So, a few new hires came on who were actually FBI agents.

Never in my wildest and darkest imaginings would I have expected my wife to be one of the two guilty parties. Didn't expect her boyfriend in the accounting department to be the other one, since up to that moment I had not a single clue that there was a boyfriend. Trusting fool that I am.

*

I paused and shook my head, wincing inwardly at a twinge of old anger. "Sorry. Don't mean to be bitter..."

"Seems you have every right." Sam reached across the table and squeezed my hand. The warmth of her brown skin against mine felt good, and somehow, reassuring. She didn't maintain the contact, looking a little self-conscious as she drew her hand back in a quick way that made it plain the impulse embarrassed her. I was sorry that she let go, but just smiled and went on with the story.

*

At any rate, when all was said and done, I found myself well off, but thoroughly burned out by betrayal at the end of a long FBI investigation and subsequent trial. I was also more restless than I've been since I was a teenager. Back then I'd have partied, used any trick in the book to get laid. This time I needed something else, something more substantial, between me and that bad experience. I felt this irresistible urge to be somewhere else, anywhere else, and so I hit the road. Packed it up, handed over the company to the new owner group, and headed first south to visit friends in San Diego, then east into the desert. It was mid-May, which might as well be summer in the Southwest, so I made it through the deserts of southern California and Arizona in a series of night drives to beat the heat. Coming from the Bay Area, that hot, dry air was hard to put up with. At times it was worth it, though. Ever seen the stars in a dark desert sky? You should do that someday. It does something good for you, deep in your soul.

Gained some altitude as I headed north and east and switched to the day shift, driving through mountains and pine forests. The desert has a fragrance that's pleasant enough, but I much prefer the scent of pine, or the breeze coming off the ocean. This time it was pines. Amazing countryside. The more I saw of it, the more I was drawn into its interior and away from civilization. Further north, then east, into northern New Mexico. Found my way to a place that seemed to say something to me, with enough elevation to support open pine forests, and took a break in my headlong flight from all that was familiar. Set up camp and watched people come and go for a couple of weeks, catching my breath as I decided where else I wanted to go.

I'd been there a week when I first spotted the dog, a furtive, frightened creature that seemed to worry the other campers more than any of the bears that paid us infrequent visits. This dog was in poor shape, undernourished, filthy, and smelling like a skunk if you were downwind of it. Many people camping there left food for the poor thing, but though he would eat, he never let anyone lay hands on him. Even underfed, he was a large example of his breed, sturdy but longer-legged than usual, with ears and tail intact. I saw him around, but paid little attention to the animal. Didn't want to get involved.

And yet, when he turned up lurking at the edge of my campsite after that first week, I felt compelled to talk to him. I didn't try to lure him in with food, on his initial visit, just addressed the nervous beast kindly, one lost soul to another. Told him it was okay, that I wouldn't hurt him, that sort of thing. He peered at me for a while, looking worn and weary, and then wandered back into the woods.

"Showed up a couple of weeks ago," the wife of the camp host told me, while she and a ranger made the rounds and lectured those doing stupid things with food in bear country. "No one can get near him."

"There was a problem, around the Memorial Day weekend, and not just here," said the ranger, whose name was Laurel. She listed off the names of several campgrounds in the area. "Dogs disappeared. There were a couple of guys showing up at the same time, driving around like they were checking campsites. We got suspicious and checked them out. The disappearances stopped happening for a while after I spoke to them. Then they reappeared and a couple more dogs went missing. This big fellow was one of them. Family stuck around looking for him for a week, but no luck."

"That must have been hard, leaving without him," I said.

"It was downright ugly, according the last folks in town to work with them trying to find the dog. I'm told one of the kids nearly needed sedation, when they left." Ranger Laurel frowned, plainly angered by the memory, and shook her head. "Yep, pretty sure it's this dog. Gawd, doesn't he look pitiful?"

"No collar and no tags," I pointed out. "Even if he decides to trust someone out here, how do you find the owners?"

"We had lost dog signs all over the place for a few weeks," Laurel said. "I'll see if any are still up. If that doesn't work, maybe he's chipped."

"Chipped?" I asked.

"Micro-chipped," she explained. "It's a little electronic tag they stick under the skin. A vet can scan it and get the dog's owner's contact information."

"We'd have to catch him first," I said as the dog faded once more into the underbrush and made it a moot point. He'd been lurking again until the camp host started talking. He clearly didn't trust her.

I didn't see the dog for a few days after that. Then one night, as I stared up through the trees to the stars and the first quarter moon, I realized I was being watched. I felt a jolt of alarm, then I realized it wasn't a bear, not even a small one. It was the dog, half concealed by bushes that were varying shades of gray in the moonlight. Only the head and shoulders of the beast were visible above the shadows beneath the shrubs. It was a somewhat spooky sight.

"Hello, there," I said, trying not to let my sudden fright change my tone of voice. "Aren't you just the very image of a lost soul?"

I'd been sipping whiskey since sundown, contemplating my recent fate, feeling a little melodramatic and more than a little sorry for myself. All of a sudden, that lost dog really felt like a kindred spirit. He sat there in the shadows, not moving a muscle, staring at me. I have no idea why I did it, unless it was the booze loosening my tongue, but I started telling him my sad story. The dog sat there, listening, as I rambled on with my tale of betrayal, now and then cocking his head to one side. "No, really, it's true," I said each time he did that.

"So, what's your story?" I asked at last. "Fall in with some bad company?"

The dog gazed at me for a moment, then stood up. For just a second, I thought he would come to me, but he turned and disappeared into the shadows.

"Easy come, easy go," I muttered. "But thanks for listening."

The next morning, surprised and pleased that I wasn't more hung over, I made coffee and a breakfast of sausage and scrambled eggs. I'd been in town the day before to resupply, and over-bought on such essentials as eggs and sausage. Needed to use the old stock first, which gave me a dozen eggs to use up while they were still good. I'd seen the dog lurking nearby already and figured I'd set the leftovers out for him. No bear risk; I'd clean up well before the sun set that evening. I assumed he would come to the food, eat it, and slink off, leaving me to do the dishes. That's how it had been with the other campers I'd spoken to about the matter, and I had no reason to believe he would turn down my offering. So, I poured coffee, piled my plate with a medley of sausage and eggs, and scraped the generous remains into a shallow pan.

Turned and found the dog barely three feet behind me, looking at the pan of still steaming food with great interest. He must really have liked scrambled eggs, I thought, considering how wary he had been of everyone else.

"Well, good morning to you, lost soul," I said.

The dog whined softly and I set the food down between us, then sat at the picnic table to eat. He made short work of my offering, and was more than willing to accept the bagel I tossed to him. I watched the poor thing as he ate, eyes occasionally rolling up to see what I was doing. When we'd both eaten what there was, he stood gazing at me, eyebrows going up and down the way dogs do, as if trying to decide what to do with me.

"Don't worry," I said. "I puzzle most of the people I meet." On impulse I held my hand down and out to him. "Poor guy. How the hell will you make out, come winter?"

The dog came to me slowly, very carefully and thoroughly smelling my hand and wrist. He was quivering with anxiety, clearly ready to bolt the instant he thought his approach to this strange human was a mistake. As big as he was, I never felt threatened. He shied away at first when I tried to touch him, then allowed me scratch between his ears. The poor dog smelled about as bad as a dog can stink. As I wondered what in the world to make of this encounter — why me, of all people? — I heard someone talking; the voices grew louder as they approached my campsite. The dog glanced toward them, then at me, and trotted back off into the brush. In a moment he was gone. I stood up and tried to see if he'd kept going or was hiding nearby, but couldn't tell.

It was Ranger Laurel, who was a tall, thin woman with short brown hair, and the spry but elderly camp host himself, sans wife. "Made a friend?" the host asked.

"Sort of," I replied. "Came to join me for

breakfast. We seemed to be making something of a connection, before you guys came along."

"Ah, sorry about that," said Laurel, who looked around for the dog, then gave it up with a shrug.

"Don't worry about it. I have no idea what I'd do with a dog, anyway."

"Still, I'm glad to see him let his guard down a little," said Laurel. "We need to see if we can get him into town before the season ends. I'd rather he came to trust someone, rather than need to trap the poor guy."

"Think someone there would take him in?" I asked.

"Permanently? Don't know," she replied with a shrug. Her tanned, weathered face wore a frown. "But our local vet says he'll put him up until we can find someone."

"Since you made more progress than we've had in weeks," said the camp host, "I'll bring over the collar and leash we picked up. If you can get that on him, and maybe take him over to my camp site...?"

"If I can collar him without having my arm ripped off, I'll walk him over to the station," I said to Laurel, a little irked at being volunteered like that. Okay, more than a little, and apparently it showed. And there was something about the way the elderly camp host volunteered to take the dog, after the hard part was done, that annoyed me.

"Don't mean to lay this on you," said Laurel. "But he did come to you." She shrugged again. "And I'll get him to the vet in town if you can manage it." Oddly enough, the camp host gave her a quick look of annoyance, but said nothing. I wondered for half a moment what might have brought that on.

"Okay, bring me the leash," I replied. "But no promises. That's a big dog and I'm not taking any chances."

"No pressure," Laurel said. "But — thanks."

"Sure."

They left and after I dealt with dirty dishes, I went down to the wooden comfort station to clean up. There was a shower in the campground and I made reluctant use of it. Cold water? Pretty sure it was snow melt just the day before. I was more or less clean when I was done, and chilled to the bone. Back in the campsite I rigged my hammock to be in the morning sun, crawled in, and let the summer sun bake the shivers out of me. Comfortably ensconced in the hammock, I tried to figure out what it was about the old guy serving as camp host that irritated me, but there was nothing I could draw a circle around and label. I quit worrying about it. I must have dozed a bit and missed the return of said host, because at some point I shifted position and saw a wide dog collar and a coiled leash on the picnic table. Also, a large bag of dog food.

"Yeah, right," I muttered, closing my eyes. I was warmed through, but the early morning sun still felt good. "Whatever."

"Whatever" whuffled at me from just a few feet to my right. I opened my eyes and looked, and found the dog standing there, watching me. The tail wagged slowly.

"Welcome back," I said. "You don't have to worry about those guys. They're on your side." I swung around and stepped out of the hammock. "In fact, they left you a couple of presents."

Going to the table, I picked up the braided leather leash and bright green woven nylon collar, then after a moment left the leash where it was and turned toward the dog with the open collar in one hand.

"Willing to bet you've seen one of these before," I said, sitting down at the table and keeping the wide collar visible in my hand. "Want to try it on for size?" I bent toward him and held out my free hand.

The dog came forward, slowly, and smelled my hand. I held the collar out to him for his inspection when he was done. It looked brand new, so I doubt he smelled any previous dog on it. I talked at him for a few minutes and was able once again to scratch the top of his head between the ears. It was warm, sitting there in the sun, and he started panting. Looking up at me with his mouth partly open in that goofy grin they all seem to have when relaxed, I was aware that the damage he might do was no laughing matter. This was a really big dog with strong jaws and a full set of healthy-looking teeth. But there was nothing in his body language that remotely hinted at a threat. Caution, yes, but we'd clearly made a connection.

"What do you think?" I asked, holding the

collar before him with both hands. "I think it would be an excellent look for you."

And leaned forward to place the collar around his neck and buckle it in place. He didn't pull back or shy away, just sat there panting rank doggy breath all over me. I sat up, patted his head and said, "Yes, sir, a very good look indeed. It's what all the well-dressed pups are wearing this summer."

Another thing that was readily apparent, sitting this close together, was how prominently his ribs were displayed down each side. I started to take a mental inventory, wonder how my supplies would hold up, when I remembered the dog food. I got up and opened it, found the pan the dog had eaten scrambled eggs from earlier, and poured what seemed an appropriate amount. The action caused him to erupt into frantic whines and whufflings, and a vocalization that sounded to my ears like "ah roo roo."

"I'll bet it's been a while." I put the pan on the ground and he plowed into it. Though I knew he must have been getting water from somewhere, I just had a feeling it would be a good way to round off the meal, so I filled a pot and set it on the ground beside him. The dog glanced at it, finished the kibble, then drank the pot of water almost dry.

Afterward, he stood there gazing at me, occasionally licking his chops, brown eyes following every move I made. I kept up the conversation, since he seemed to respond well to hearing a kindly voice. Just once I looked at the leash, and again thought better of it. He showed no sign of being ready or willing to run back off into the bush, and if he objected to the leash, I very much doubted I could handle him by myself. Better to let him make his own decisions for the moment. As I was considering all this and examining him, little details made themselves known. There was a trio of half-healed welts on one hip, several engorged ticks, and redness in one eye that spoke of irritation, if not infection. To say nothing of his general odor.

"Buddy, you're one hell of mess," I muttered, patting a filthy shoulder. "Not judging you, of course. I wouldn't be doing this good, under the circumstances. But I've got an idea."

I went to the old, dark red SUV I was driving and switched from ordinary sandals to a pair meant for walking in wet places. The stream running past the campground was less than a quarter of a mile away, and I headed down the path leading from my campsite to the main trail to the creek, urging him to follow. The dog looked puzzled for a moment, then trotted after me as if we'd been walking together all his life. And again, I kept up the chatter, as if my voice was some sort of connecting device, a leash made of words. Which, in a way, I suppose it was.

There were a few people with binoculars on the far side of the stream, which was no more than a dozen feet across. Their attention was fixed on something fluttering around near the top of a willow tree on their side of the stream. Clear water rippled and cast bright points of reflected sunlight as it flowed over a bed of gravel and sand. The stream on our side was clothed in bedraggled grass, vegetation clinging grimly to the shores in defiance of constant foot traffic. Beyond the grass were leafy shrubs heavy with sweet-scented white flowers. Taller trees were well back from where we were. No one was fishing the stream, which was a stroke of luck. I waded in, deliberately splashing as I went, then turned to look back when it was up to my bare knees and swirling slowly and gently around my legs. Warm sunshine made a pleasant contrast to the chilly water. The dog was standing on the shore, watching me, head tilted to one side as if puzzled.

"Well, come on!" I said over the sound of the water. "It's not that deep."

He seemed to come to a decision, gathered himself, and in a single lunge landed halfway between dry land and my position. Made quite a splash, and then cracked me up as he started romping around in the water like some crazed two-year-old. He went around me, from water that just covered his paws to midstream where he swam without apparent concern for the modest current. I moved to somewhat shallower water and splashed at him. The dog came to me, panting and clearly delighted. Tail wag? The whole dog was wagging. I started splashing water up over him and rubbing off the mud and tiny bits of debris in his fur. His only reaction to these ministrations was to gently nibble my ear a couple of times.

I couldn't do anything about the ticks then and there, but I could deal with that back in camp. In the meantime, I did what I could to clean him up, checked those welts on his hip — damned if they didn't look like claw marks — and generally marveled at the speed with which he'd given me his trust. Would not have expected it, and although I still didn't want to take on the responsibility long-term, that sudden trust did feel good.

*

"For someone who isn't much of a dog person, you sure handled the big pup well."

"I grew up with dogs. Raised puppies, watched them grow old and — what was that saying? Watched them pass over the bridge? Went out into the adult world and just never had time for one."

Sam gave me a guilty look and said, "Sorry, I shouldn't have interrupted you."

"Feel free," I said. And truly didn't mind at all.

*

We went back to the campsite, and the warm air dried us both off by the time we got back. I pulled a jar of petroleum jelly out of my first aid kit and applied it liberally to every tick

I could find. They can't breathe through that stuff and drop off their victim trying to get air. The dog sat there as patient as can be, making no objections, and from time to time licking my hand or arm. As I worked, I become ever more strongly aware that, even after a swim and a quick scrub in the river, he desperately needed a real bath, with soap.

I ran out of ticks before I ran out of stuff to smother them, gave the dog a pat on the shoulder, and said, "So, what do we do next?"

The dog yawned, stretched, and ambled casually away from my campsite a few yards and took a dump.

"I'll try not to take that personally." I had a small shovel for digging latrines while free camping, and made use of it. Some of my neighbors were already casting worried glances, no doubt due to the intimidating sight of what they must have thought of as a potentially dangerous animal on the loose closer to their camp sites than had been the case. Didn't want to give them anything more to fret about.

The dog came back, found the shade under my hammock and flopped down on the dusty ground with a sigh. He didn't fall completely asleep, and now and then a noise would bring his head up for a wary look around, but he seemed otherwise calm and relaxed. I sat on the picnic table, pleased by what I'd managed to accomplish, while at the same time not being at all sure about what to do next. To get him to the ranger station would surely require use of the leash. How would he react to feeling restrained? Or about being loaded into a vehicle? I was in no hurry to find out.

« 3 »

We just sort of hung out together for the rest of that pleasantly warm day. Anyone walking by, not knowing any better, would have assumed the dog was right where he belonged. As the afternoon wore on, I cooked dinner and gave the dog another bowl of food. I was trying to be cautious about feeding him — didn't want him getting sick from too much, too soon after his time of near starvation — but he seemed able to handle whatever I gave him.

There are signs all over the region declaring it "bear country." They were displayed prominently in the campground. If you're smart, you cook and eat early when camping in bear country, before the bears become active for the night. Fortunately, this was before the most recent drought cycle took hold in the western states, so the bears weren't starving and desperate enough to be aggressive in campgrounds. Nowadays, having food with you at all amounts to having a target on your back.

That particular summer the only people who had trouble with bears were the ones who did truly stupid things with food, and they generally suffered only property damage and occasionally the fright of their lives. I'd seen two bears by then, or the same bear twice, and then only from a distance. Both times the animal was in the campsite of someone learning a lesson. I knew they wandered through the campground early in the evening, and on into the night, and had even heard one huffing and chuffing in the dark, but that's as far as it had gone. I was sufficiently unconcerned about local bears that I spent most nights dozing in the hammock. I always ate dinner in the late afternoon, while the sun was still up, and had everything cleaned and stowed away before dark. It was simple fare with a couple of beers when I was feeling mellow. Stronger stuff when memories intruded, as they did far too often.

After eating, cleaning, and putting things safely away that night, I popped open a captain's chair and settled down to read one of the books I'd brought along. The late afternoon faded into evening. Swirls of sunset color made a backdrop for the ponderosa pines around me. The faintest of breezes brought the scent of pine and something being barbecued. I could hear other campers talking and laughing. One of my neighbors played his guitar each evening; didn't mind it a bit, as the lad was quite good. I suppose the beer in my hand was technically a violation of the food rule I mentioned, but apparently it wasn't as effective as bear bait as cooking a meal over a stove or charcoal. A bait someone nearby was advertising on the evening breeze.

This had become my routine, since setting up camp. Reading a bit until it grew too dark, then sitting alone with my thoughts, sorting things out, enjoying a measure of peace. Yes, memories intruded on some evenings — okay, most evenings — but they seemed easier to cope with in that setting. California was a long way off by then. It was almost as if the trial and divorce had happened to someone else. Almost.

This time there was a dog involved; he seemed to think it was a fine plan, and was content to doze at my feet. Now and then he would come halfway up, staring in the direction of some sound I hadn't heard. More often than not he would settle back down, but twice he surged to his feet, tense and alert. I peered into the gathering twilight, saw nothing, and gave him a pat on the rump, saying the sorts of things one does to a nervous dog. Each time he settled back down after giving me a long, hard look. I was apparently clueless regarding dangers in the dark, but I was the human and we're always in charge, right? I didn't react, so he just settled back down, even if he remained watchful. No doubt such caution was part of the reason he was still alive. His gaze followed me as I got up to turn on the lantern, turning it down low to make it easier on the eyes, and to conserve the battery. It never became completely dark with a nearly waxing moon shining high in the south. It was a warm, beautiful summer night.

When I could no longer keep my eyes open, I prepared the hammock for the night's sleep. The dog's head came up as he watched me as I did that. His tail thumped the ground if I looked his way, but he otherwise stayed as he was, to all appearances calm and content with his current situation. I wondered briefly if I should secure him to something with the leash, or lock him in the truck, but for some reason it just felt unnecessary. Having decided to trust me, the dog gave no sign he was restless, and I didn't want to give him a reason *not* to trust me. Apparently sleeping in my campsite felt far more secure than whatever safety and shelter he'd found in the woods on previous nights.

It was inevitable, of course. I'd no more than settled for the night when those beers caught up with me. "Idiot," I muttered. The dog peered up at me in the moonlight. "Not you, bud. I always do this. Really should know better." I strapped on the hiking sandals and shuffled off to the restrooms, not bothering with a flashlight. I knew the way and the moonlight was more than adequate. No surprise, the dog got up and followed silently along. There were lights of various sorts in the campsites scattered around me, including the comforting flicker of campfires, but there wasn't another soul in sight at the comfort station when I arrived. When I came back out I realized immediately that the dog had wandered off. For a moment I was caught between feeling alarmed and annoyed, then I saw him a few yards up the trail toward the campsite, sniffing the trunk of a tree.

"Thought you'd abandoned me," I said as he turned and trotted back toward me.

Less than ten feet from me the dog stopped and froze. A sound came out of him, the prelude to a growl. It was followed at once by the real thing, and that was followed by nothing less than a snarl. His head lowered and he set himself as if about to charge.

"Hey, buddy," I said, more than a little alarmed. "Hey, take it easy. I thought we were friends here?"

The dog's growl rose in volume and by the light of the moon I could see the gleam of bared teeth. The growl was punctuated by the short barks of a dog about to go to war. I started to take a step back, wondering if I could get up the nearest tree in time, when I finally realized that he wasn't looking at me. He was looking past me.

"Oh, shit!" I did not turn, not right away. My heart felt like it was beating under my chin. "It's behind me, isn't it?"

The dog never took his eyes from whatever drew his ire. I turned slowly and, sure enough, there was a bear on the trail with us. It stood there much too close for comfort, a dark mass with no real details to be seen, just a shadow in the moonlight exuding a sense of size and power. Just once I caught the gleam of moonlight in its eyes. It took a step forward, and then paused as the dog barked twice. I stepped off the trail, hoping the bear was just passing through. It didn't seem to be challenging us, just waiting to see what we would do. I had good reason to assume this was all about right-of-way. I'd been in a similar situation some years before, in bear country of a different state, and yielding that right-of-way had been enough. I held my breath and hoped that was all it would take this time. But the dog didn't know the rule, and he seemed frozen in place. With short, stiff steps, he put himself between me and the bear, then held his ground.

"Hey! Come here!"

The dog did not respond immediately; I stood there absolutely still, almost afraid to breath. Finally, without taking his eyes from the bear, the dog moved toward me, walking slowly backward. His head was low and he was ready to fight, but miracle of miracles, came when I called, and then moved further off the trail when I spoke to him again. It was excruciating, we gave ground so slowly, but at last we backed our way across some invisible line and the bear turned away from us. It sauntered away, with an occasional backwards glance.

It sometimes works that way. Give the bear the right-of-way, let it have the trail. Sometimes. We were lucky that night. If the dog hadn't come when I called, the bear would have killed him. Might have attacked me, too, and we all know what happens to a bear that injures or kills a human being. But that night everyone got lucky, and everyone went on with their lives.

Went on with my life? Well, yes, but from that night onward, nothing was ever quite the same for me. I didn't know it right away, but my aimless wandering was done, and I was no longer traveling alone.

« 4 »

That the nature of my trip had changed became abundantly obvious the next day.

To start with, Laurel drove up to my campsite that morning with a copy of the lost dog poster she had mentioned. Actually, it was little better than a notice, a bit of eight and a half by eleven paper, ragged along the bottom edge, with a faded black-and-white reproduction of a family portrait dominating two thirds of it. A man who looked to be in his late thirties, a woman who might have been younger, four children, and a very familiar-looking dog. According to the brief message pleading for his return, the dog's name was Toby.

"There's no contact information on this," I pointed out.

Laurel, seated at the picnic table with me

and enjoying an offered cup of coffee, did not look up from the dog head she was scratching. There was a look of amazement on her face. "This is hard to figure. Couldn't get near him before, and now, with you sitting here and telling him it's okay, I'm allowed it scratch itches. And no, there isn't any contact information. They set that up so you tore off little bits along the bottom with a phone number printed on it. Those are all long gone."

"Well, handy as it is to know what to call the big guy," I said, "this isn't a lot of help."

"Maybe not by itself," she said. "But I remember they were in touch with the veterinarian in town, hoping someone would bring Toby there. Now that we have him, and he sure looks like the dog in that photo, we can take him into town and give that microchip thing a try. Dr. Nelson is more of a horse doctor, works with the ranchers hereabouts, but he's really good with dogs, too. His wife is an absolute wizard with them. Their neighbors call her 'the dog whisperer.' I believe he actually went out and tried to help them find Toby. At any rate, that picture should remind him of who these guys were. Willing to bet he can get hold of them."

The unspoken assumption was that I'd be taking Toby to the veterinarian for that purpose. I almost objected, but decided that having gone this far, there was no reason to balk at taking him into town. I was assuming at that moment that the local vet would take him in. "It's a weekday, so that clinic is probably open," I said instead.

"It is," she said. "I checked."

"All right, I'll see if old Toby is up for a ride, and pay that vet a visit."

"I'll call them from the station and give 'em a heads up." Ranger Laurel paused, then added, "His name is Frank Nelson, by the way."

"Sounds like a plan," I replied.

"And thanks for doing this," she added with a warm smile. "Really appreciate the help."

*

I get the impression you and that ranger hit it off pretty well," Sam observed.

"We did," I agreed. "Liked her quite a bit, and I'm pretty sure she was spending more time at my site than she really needed to. But I just wasn't up for even a brief relationship at the time. In fact, the possibility that she'd taken an interest didn't occur until after I left. My head was in that kind of mess at the time."

"Been there." Sam grimaced, a look that did her no favors. "I'll always wonder how things might have turned out, but, well, you know..." She shook her head and sighed.

"Oh, I do know, but I've learned the hard way not to dwell on what might have been," I replied. "Most people cross your path when they do, the way they do, but only briefly, because that's where you both are in life, if you know what I mean. Trying to hang on to such

moments rarely seems to end well."

"It can be a hard lesson, that's for sure,"
said Sam.

A customer paused just then and asked
about the dog. He listened as Sam gave him
details on the animal's size and history, then
frowned and wished her luck in finding the
dog a home. Sam sighed and looked sad as the
customer wandered off. I think that's when I
finally decided.

There was a tag on the cage that had the
name "Moe" printed on it. There was a word
on the other side. I flipped it to see what that
word was. Adopted.

I left the tag flipped, and went on with my
story.

It was worth it for the look on Sam's face.

*

I packed up my modest kit before making
the drive, having learned the hard way that
forest service campgrounds were anything but
crime free. The site was reserved for three more
days, and I had every intention of returning
and finishing my unplanned stay there. Toby
was no problem when it came to taking that
ride. I put the collar and leash on him and led
him to the driver's side rear door. He hopped
up onto the seat without any hesitation and
spent the drive time peering through the
window or over my shoulder. It was an
uneventful drive to town, and with the

directions Laurel provided, I found my way to the veterinarian's office without any problem. Of course, the town was small, and I'd have run out of town before I could get lost in it.

The pine scent of the outside air was replaced by the smell of disinfectant as I led Toby through the glass door. I've never been in a veterinary clinic that smelled any different. The waiting room was small and pretty bare, with just a couple of padded chairs flanking a large window and a few photos of horses on the walls. I was met there by a slender young woman with black hair, wearing a loose blue smock and brown slacks. She acknowledged getting that call from Laurel and used an intercom to summon the vet. A moment later Dr. Nelson, a tall and powerfully-built man with a deep tan, wearing a white jacket and jeans, came into the lobby, drying his hands on a towel. Toby let out a deep whuffle of dog speak and approached the man, head down and tail wagging vigorously. The vet did indeed remember Toby, and Toby clearly remembered the man.

"Hey, buddy, how the hell are ya?" His voice was surprisingly soft for a man built as he was. He slung the towel over his shoulder and went down on one knee. "Didn't think we'd ever see *you* around here again."

"You're Dr. Nelson?" I asked.

"That's me," he said.

"So, this really is the dog in that flier?" The vet's immediate familiarity with the dog made it seem more than likely.

"He was a patient," Dr. Nelson said with a nod. The vet was in the process of scratching various itchy places. "He ate something he shouldn't have when the family was on the road. They camped near here while we treated him. Nothing serious, as I recall. Had him ready to romp in a couple of days." He gave a sturdy canine hip a solid thump. Toby just panted and wagged.

"So, what do you know about him getting lost?" I asked.

The vet stood up, frowning and frankly looking pissed off, not a comfortable expression to see on a man I would not have crossed for any money. "We apparently had dog thieves in the area a while back. How they were doing it, I don't know for sure. Maybe they used drugged meat as bait. Two young guys were seen in area campgrounds, acting as if they were looking for a campsite, and sometime after they moved on dogs would go missing. Usually little ones. We have one reliable report of someone seeing one of these guys carrying what looked like a small dog back to their car."

"How did they manage to get away with that?" I asked. I couldn't imagine leaving a dog unattended in a campsite.

"People get careless, at times," Nelson replied. "And people are sometimes stupid. Unfortunately, a few dogs paid for it this time."

"And this fellow?" I asked.

"His family left him in their van when they went to a presentation at the ranger station,"

Nelson replied. "It was evening, sun was down, so they felt safe doing it. Locking the doors seemed safe enough, but when they came back the van had been broken into and the dog was gone. How they didn't hear him barking at strangers breaking into their vehicle beats me. Just as puzzling is how they managed to subdue this big fellow and run off with him." Dr. Nelson looked down at Toby. "Can't help thinking he gave them a nasty surprise, when he made good his escape."

"Dog thieves," I muttered, looking down at Toby. "To what purpose?"

"Our Sheriff thinks they're connected to a dogfight ring."

That set me back for a moment. "Isn't that sort of thing illegal?"

"Damned right, it is." The vet was glowering in a way that almost prompted me to take a step back. "They probably wanted Toby to train for fighting. The smaller dogs..." He stopped talking rather abruptly.

"Were these bastards ever caught?" I asked.

"Not yet," Dr. Nelson said, shaking his head. "Our one witness recognized the man she saw when the local gas station ran security camera images for her. We got descriptions of the other guy. It was definitely the two men who aroused Laurel's suspicions. Sheriff tapped into some sort of law enforcement network to check these guys out, and then just stopped talking about it. At a guess, I'd say there's more to these characters than dog snatching." His gaze shifted to his employee, who was by then back behind the reception counter; she appeared to be busy behind a computer.

"Guess you're the lucky one," I said, looking down and patting Toby on the head. Inside I was cringing. I mean, the thought... "So, can you get in touch with his owners?"

"Sure can," he replied. And then grimaced for a moment. "They're in Illinois."

I looked down at Toby. "You're a bit hefty to send out by air mail, bud." I was about to ask how the dog's return might be managed when the receptionist spoke.

"Doctor Nelson, look who just pulled into the parking lot."

The vet looked out the big front window. "Well, son of a bitch. Laurel and Sheriff Schofield must have been right about these two working with the camp host."

"There was a call not half an hour ago from Laurel telling me the camp host was talking to these guys, shortly after she sent the gentleman to us." She pulled a phone from her smock as she spoke and waved it toward the window. "They're going to walk right into it, just as I thought." She made a very quick call. I couldn't hear what she said, but it sounded tight and professional.

A Camaro had parked one space over from my SUV. The car wasn't new, and once upon a time might have been bright red. There were two men inside who did not seem to be in a particular hurry to get out.

"The camp host?" I asked.

"It's definitely not Laurel who spilled the beans," Dr. Nelson replied. He looked both nervous and angry.

Damn it all, what the hell had I gotten myself into?

"Sir, why don't you lead Toby this way," the receptionist said. "You two can stay out of sight back here." She indicated a swinging door that led into the exam area.

I tried to comply, but Toby became an inanimate object at that point, staring out the window as the men in the Camaro climbed out. I spoke his name, tugged and then pulled on the leash, but only got him halfway there before he froze, eyes riveted on the front door.

"Did you call...?" Dr. Nelson started to say.

"The Sheriff is on his way."

"Good." The doctor was definitely anxious about something. His jaw was clenched as tight as his fists. Seeing this did not give me a good feeling.

The receptionist turned to me and motioned to the doorway into the clinic. "Sir, I need you to take the dog out of here right now."

I gave his shoulder an insistent nudge and got him all the way to the door, but it was too late. The bell jangled over the door and two dudes walked in, just a moment too late to put Toby out of sight. The dog turned, saw them, and froze again, staring back into the lobby. I pulled the leash, but he held his ground. I might have been able to budge him with a front-end loader. Just as he had with the bear,

43

he planted himself between me and the newcomers, and emitted a low, rumbling growl. As for the two dudes, their car might have been something of a stereotype, but there was nothing about these guys that screamed "criminal." They were both tall, fairly young, in good shape and dressed casually, but cleanly, in jeans and T-shirts, one pronouncing his loyalty to the Baltimore Orioles, the other advertising the fact that the wearer had survived a rock concert I'd never heard of. Although it was plenty warm enough, they wore jackets, one denim, the other leather. They wore baseball caps, one over dark hair — leather jacket dude — and the other over a shaved head — denim jacket dude — with logos too faded to read with a casual glance. Could have been just a couple of guys down from one of the campgrounds.

"Help you, gentlemen?" the receptionist asked.

"Someone said a dog looking like one we lost was brought down from the campground," said denim jacket dude. "Was hoping..."

"That's him, right there," said leather jacket dude. "Damn, didn't think we'd see him again."

They sounded unnervingly sincere, but Toby wasn't buying it. His stance was identical to the way he'd been the night of the bear, and the low rumbling growl became an angry snarl. He definitely recognized these dudes, and was not happy to see them again. But he wasn't retreating.

"Need to see some proof of ownership," Dr. Nelson said. All things considered, he sounded wary, but otherwise calm.

The growl grew louder, clearly audible, and ended in another snarl. "You sure about this, guys?" I asked. "'Cause I don't think he's at all happy to see you."

"Well, sure, he's upset," said denim jacket dude.

"He'll get over it," leather jacket dude assured us, smiling.

I tried to nudge Toby in the direction of the door. Might as well have tried to shove a fire hydrant. The growl continued, growing rapidly in volume and complexity. I wondered what chance I had to hold him back if he went after these two men, both of whom were giving Toby decidedly nervous glances. I had a deeply anxious feeling about how such an event would go, if I couldn't hold on. I put my hand on his head and told him to take it easy, that everything would be okay. The dog under my hand was vibrating.

Through the window I saw two vehicles pull in behind the Camaro, both of them from the county's sheriff's department.

"Whatever," said Dr. Nelson. "I still need proof you own the dog. Vaccination record, family photo, anything like that?"

"You sure you want to put us to that much trouble, doc?" asked leather jacket dude. He reached around to the small of his back, as if scratching an itch.

"Don't," said the receptionist.

There was something about her voice. We all looked her way, and everyone froze. The woman had a large handgun aimed at the nearest of the two dudes; her aim was rock steady and her face was blank of expression. Leather jacket dude very carefully brought his arm back around and held his empty hands in plain view. Denim jacket dude did the same.

"Excellent," she said. "Both of you very slowly put your hands on your heads. And I mean on top of your heads, right where I can see them." The two dudes looked at each other, both alarmed and clearly pissed off, but they complied with her demand and made no sudden moves.

"The hell?" I said. Toby, at least, had stopped growling, but watched it all with wary eyes.

"She's FBI," said Dr. Nelson, stepping over to stand with Toby between us.

"Special Agent Soren," she said. "And you boys are under arrest."

The door opened again and both dudes glanced over their shoulders in time to see the sheriff and two deputies come through, guns drawn. "Nice," said the sheriff. With a nod he sent his deputies forward, and in short order the dudes were disarmed — both had handguns stuck in pants waists, hidden by their jackets — placed in handcuffs, and had heard their rights. In glum silence they allowed themselves to be led outside and tucked away in patrol cars, one in each.

Agent Soren's weapon vanished in the

meantime. I never did learn where she had it hidden.

"The FBI goes after dog thieves?" I asked. I was amazed by how calm I sounded, considering I could feel my heartbeat making my scalp pulse.

She grinned at me, obviously pleased with the way things had gone down. "I would if they let me make it a priority," she replied. "But no, the dog thing is the tip of the iceberg. These two and the family they were working for are into some seriously bad things. I can't say exactly what, of course. This is just a side hustle, although apparently it pays pretty well when dog fighting is the boss's hobby. They were probably paid well, and in advance, for this dog. But he got away from them. When the rangers told me that you'd rescued this big fella, I figured these morons would try something like this, and Dr. Nelson's clinic was the obvious site for luring them in. The chance to grab those two was too good to resist. And I must thank Dr. Nelson for his cooperation."

"It was a genuine pleasure," said Dr. Nelson as he wiped perspiration from his brow with the back of his shaking hand.

"You and that ranger," I said, trying to hold my voice steady. In that moment of the adrenaline surge I couldn't for the life of me remember her name. "You set me up for this."

"Well, yes, we did," Soren replied, looking sheepish. "I really did want you out of here, and out of a risky situation. Big doggo here had other ideas." And she flashed Toby a grin.

"Fortunately, the Sheriff and I had this all worked out in advance."

"Sorry about that," I said. "I did try."

"Nothing to worry about now."

The Sheriff came to stand beside Agent Soren. He looked old enough to be her father and then some, and her head barely came above his shoulder, but there was something about the woman that made it seem he couldn't possibly loom over her. "Just got word that your boys nailed the rest of them up at their cabin."

"Great news," Soren said. "And nice work on your part here. Impeccable timing, sir."

"One of those times when we're more than happy to oblige," he replied. He sounded pleased, but didn't so much as smile.

"It was certainly an interesting thing to witness," I said. "Speaking of which, I've apparently just become one, haven't I?"

Soren laughed and said, "Don't worry, sir. I just need a signed statement from you regarding what you saw here, and some contact information. We pretty much have everything we need on this gang already."

"That's good," I said. "I was planning to be on the road for a while. Might make me difficult to track down."

"Oh, we'd find you if we needed to," she replied with a smirk.

I saw no reason to doubt it. And as it turned out, they did so, eventually.

Special Agent Soren and the Sheriff left the clinic and I turned to find the good doctor bent at the waist, idly scratching Toby between his ears.

"You okay?" I asked, still trying to pull my own heart rate down to normal.

"I am now." He let out a sigh that turned into a tight, nervous laugh, and glanced up at me. "Damn, but that was no fun at all! Welcome to the wild, wild west."

"Look at him," I said as Toby stuck his nose up and nuzzled my still shaking hand. "You'd never guess we'd just been in the middle of — that!"

"He was ready to be the middle of it," Dr. Nelson replied. "I think we were a heartbeat away from seeing just what an angry pittie is capable of."

"Is he really a pit bull?" I asked. "Sort of looks like one, but..."

"From the tail and the ears, I'm guessing there's a lab somewhere in there. Whatever he's made of, he struck me as a remarkable dog, the short time I had him here." Dr. Nelson went back down on one knee and gave one of Toby's ears a gentle tug. "You know, you can tell he was someone's puppy from the very beginning. Part of a family."

"What do you mean?"

"Never had his ears or his tail docked." Toby turned his head and licked the side of Nelson's face. "Yes, you do remember me, don't you?"

"So, about this 'someone,'" I prompted, eager to put that bizarre incident behind me.

"Laurel was right, I have their contact

information," he replied. "It's been more than a month, so they'll certainly be surprised to hear from me."

"Well, it'll be good news, even if it hands them the logistical challenge of getting him home," I muttered.

"First step in getting that done is letting them know we have him safe and sound." He straightened, looked at his watch and frowned. "Couple of hours of time difference — someone might be home, this time of day."

"Worst case, we leave a message," I said.

"Right." He went to the door, locked it, and flipped the sign to "Closed," then headed through the doorway Agent Soren had wanted me to use, waving a hand at me to indicate I should follow. I did, and Toby trotted along beside me without a moment's hesitation. Down a short hallway and past a door on each side, presumably leading to exam rooms, then into a small, tidy but windowless office at the end of the hall. Dr. Nelson sat behind the desk and started tapping at a keyboard. "I'd offer you a drink," he said as he called up whatever file he sought, "but we're both likely to be driving soon."

"Too bad," I said. "My nerves could use one right now." I took the only other chair in the room, and Toby sat patiently beside me, looking around.

As I peered at the books lining one wall, all of them references on animal health, Dr. Nelson said, "You and me both. We'll have one later. Ah, there we are." He peered at the computer screen, then picked up a cell phone on the desk and pressed buttons.

"Hey, boyo," I said to Toby. "We're about to make some people really happy. Your people."

"It's ringing," Nelson said. "Yes, hello, this is Dr. Frank Nelson, way over here in New Mexico. Mrs. Vernon? Good, glad I caught you at home." He took the phone away from his ear and turned on its speaker app. From that point I heard the other side of the conversation.

A woman's voice, sounding rather small and remote, came from the phone. "Dr. Nelson? I'm almost afraid to ask what prompts you to call."

"Only good news, Mrs. Vernon. Someone found Toby."

"What?"

"He's safe, he appears well, and he is sitting in my office as we speak, along with the gentleman who rescued him."

What was heard then over the phone was a jumbled combination of startled laughter, disbelief, weeping, and then more laughter. Not much was actually said, but a great deal was communicated, and in a very short time. Toby listened with what looked like polite interest; if he had any idea who we were talking to, it didn't show. When Mrs. Vernon had calmed down enough to manage coherent speech, it registered on her that we were in New Mexico, and she was not. "Oh, my god! How do we do this? We want him home, of course. How's that to be done?"

You know that movie where the hobbit

suddenly decides he just has to go on the adventure, and goes racing off into the wild? One of those moments rose up and seized me, just then. I would never have predicted it before it happened, but a thing needed doing and — there I was. "Mrs. Vernon? Hello, I'm Paul Ford, the guy who reeled Toby in. I'm on an extended road trip, headed east, and I intended to stop in Chicago eventually anyway. I'll bring Toby home to you, if that's okay?"

"Oh, my god! There's no way we could ask that of you."

"You didn't ask," I pointed out. "I offered."

Dr. Nelson was watching me as I spoke to Toby's person, his facial expression unreadable.

"I don't know what to say," Mrs. Vernon replied. "That's so incredibly generous. But — god, I need to talk to Jim. It would be just like him to jump on a plane and fly there tonight. Oh, we've missed our big boy so much!" Just like that she went from sounding like she was near tears to clearly crying as she spoke.

"You should definitely do that," Dr. Nelson said. "Talk to your family before making any decisions. Then get in touch with me. Do you still have my card?"

"Uh, sure, somewhere," she replied, sniffling. "And I have this number on my phone now."

"Just in case you don't find that card, here's my home number." He gave it to her and made sure she had it right. "That's the emergency number on my card, if you find it.

It's what I give the ranchers and farmers hereabouts, so it's okay to call whenever it's convenient. I always answer. Actually, it'll be later for you folks than me, so don't worry about the hour. Talk to your family about Mr. Ford's offer, then call me back this evening."

"Okay, we'll do that. We'll be in touch. Oh, thank you!" She repeated the thanks several times and was crying again when the connection ended.

Dr. Nelson looked at me from across the desk, one eyebrow raised. "Seriously?"

I shrugged and said, "Why not? I have the time and freedom to do whatever I want these days. Sold my share of the company and have nothing holding me back at the moment." That prompted a puzzled frown. "Look up Celestial Graphics and Effects and add my name."

"Oh, *that* Paul Ford," he said a moment later. Dr. Nelson relaxed visibly. "There's a news piece here about you selling out and disappearing from the Bay Area."

"It's was time to do something new," I said with a shrug, hoping that would be enough. To my relief, he hadn't noticed any news items about the arrest and prosecution of my ex-wife. "That's why I'm on the road. Sorting things out and trying to decide what to do next."

"Okay, then." Dr. Nelson smiled and lowered his eyes, looking at the dog. "Toby, my lad, you are one lucky pup. Damned lucky! Now, let's take a closer look at you and make sure things are as good as they seem."

We went into one of the exam rooms,

where Dr. Nelson weighed Toby, took his temperature — using some sort of device he poked into the ear — and listened to his heartbeat and breathing with a stethoscope. He looked very closely at the half-healed scars on Toby's hip, and determined they posed no threat to his health, there being no sign of infection. The reddened eye worried him, so he gave Toby antibiotics and a vitamin complex injection, just to be safe.

"Dr. Nelson, what do you suppose clawed him like that?" I asked.

"Probably a bobcat," he replied. "And call me Frank."

"A bobcat went after him?" I asked.

"That's just a guess," he replied with a shrug. "The marks are about the right size and spacing. They may have tangled over something both of them wanted to eat. Probably bobcat. Can't have been a cougar."

"Why not?"

Frank shrugged and said, "If it had been a cougar, the two of you wouldn't have met."

« 5 »

*

"Good God, you didn't put that part in the weblog!" Sam was wide-eyed, clearly aghast.

"Couldn't," I replied. I'd looked around to make sure no one had been in earshot when I told of that particular episode. The cashier had gone off to show a customer which aisle contained cat scratch posts. The customer doing the asking had been rather loud. "Probably shouldn't ever, even though the bastards were all successfully prosecuted and are currently doing their time." I shrugged. "Horrible people, really. Cocaine smuggling, human trafficking, other things. They were meeting others of their sort out there in the middle of nowhere, hoping to avoid notice. That didn't work out too well for them. I doubt *it remained a secret with the locals. Dr. Nelson lives in a really small town. But it isn't something I'm comfortable broadcasting. I never want any of that crowd connecting me with their downfall, if you know what I mean."*

Sam made a zipping motion over her lips, then said, "But you told Toby's people?"

"The adults in the household, yes. Just in case."

Sam whistled softly and shook her head. "That's all pretty heavy. Speaking of heavy, from the pictures I saw of Toby, that must have been frightening, having him that tense."

"Tense? Well, you could call it that. I was more afraid of what the dog might do than I was of the criminals." I looked at the dog in the cage and considered again the size of the animal, comparable to Toby, then shrugged off inevitable doubts. My decision was made. "If he'd gotten away from me — but he just stood his ground and made his displeasure known. Come to think of it, that probably distracted them at just the right moment. So, it all worked out."

*

Frank made a quick call home to warn his wife that he was sending a couple of guests home ahead of him. He turned the speaker off for that call, but from the self-deprecating laughter on his side of it I was pretty sure mine was not an isolated incident. I doubt the fact that one guest was a dog surprised her either, all things considered. I put up a token argument at the offer of their guest house for the night, but Frank pointed out he would need me, and Toby, on hand when the Vernon family made their call. My time as a happy camper had just come to an end in any case, so staying in town did make sense. Frank gave me directions to his home at the edge of town. "I don't have any appointments this afternoon, so I'll follow along as soon as I've locked the place up."

"What if someone shows up needing your services?" I asked.

"The emergency number is on the door," he replied. "And I live close by. Now, Patty will mind our kids when you get there. But keep Toby's leash firmly in hand until she says otherwise, okay?"

"Will do."

"I'll be all of ten or fifteen minutes behind you."

"Got it. And thanks." I shook his hand, led Toby out to my SUV, and hit the road.

I'd say it was a short drive from that tiny clinic to the Nelson residence, but in a town that small everything is a short drive on graded dirt roads. Houses were widely spaced and variously landscaped, although hollyhocks and sunflowers seemed a common theme. It may have taken me ten minutes, but even then, only took that long because I managed to drive past the place and had to turn around and backtrack. The family was all at the split rail fence waiting, having apparently noticed my slow pass the first time, when I'd been unsure of where exactly I was. A tall woman with sun-bleached brown hair waved at me. She had three kids to her right, and two dogs on the left; both of them looked like shepherd mixes. Everyone except the dogs wore T-shirts and jeans, with the expected variation in colors and logo. The woman was smiling as I parked and got out, leaving Toby in the front seat to watch through a half-open window. He managed to stick his head out the window, and it seemed he liked what he was seeing, the way his tail was rearranging the clutter I usually drive with.

"Mrs. Nelson?" I asked.

The smile widened to a grin. "Patty," she corrected.

"Paul Ford," I said.

"Glad to meet you," she replied. "These are the kids Frank surely mentioned." Glancing at her children she reeled off their names, Amy, Jeff, and Pete. Looking to the left she added the names Lance and Percy. All the kids said hello, either by speaking — two-legged sorts — or by wagging in the case of the furry ones. "And that would be Toby in the truck. He seems happy to be here."

"He does, indeed," I said. The steady thump of a stout tail wagging was easily heard.

"He wants to come out and play," said her youngest child, Pete.

My normally cautious nature finally found its voice. "You know, I'm not really all that familiar with this dog. No idea how he'll really react to your pups."

"Only one way to find out." She told her kids to stay put and let herself out through the front gate. Her dogs started to whine, though whether from eagerness or anxiety I couldn't tell. Both wagged furiously — which isn't always as reliable as some folks think — but neither were they rolling their eyes in that way dogs do when stressed.

*

"Whale eyes," Sam said.

"So, it does have a name, then?"

"Yep. Sure sign of an anxiously unhappy dog."

"Toby only did that once, early in the trip," I said. "The bear, the dudes, other things — he just narrowed his eyes and got ready to deal."

"That's because he felt he was in control of the situation."

"He probably wasn't wrong. Anyway..."

*

She went to the side of my SUV and held a hand up to the partly open window. "Hey, there, Toby boy. Long time, no see. Remember me, do you?" Toby obliged by slobbering all over the offered hand. "He remembers. Go ahead and let him out," she said.

"You've met?"

Patty nodded. "I usually run the front desk of the clinic. That FBI agent you met was, uh, covering for me. Sorry I missed seeing that all work out."

"I'd gladly have traded places with you, had I known. People pointing guns at each other near me isn't my idea of a good time." Speaking of the incident in bright warm sunlight, feeling a cool, fragrant breeze, rendered the memory shockingly unreal.

"Someone drew a gun?" Patti asked quietly, that sort of quiet to a voice that belies a tightly restrained reaction. "Frank didn't mention that."

"He didn't?" I replied.

"No."

"It was the agent and the Sheriff and his deputies," I explained. "And they had everything under control."

"I'm sure they did."

I silently apologized to Frank for my indiscretion, and hoped I would have a chance to warn him of it before he was alone with his wife.

I complied with her suggestion to let Toby out of the SUV, after first attaching the leash and making sure Toby couldn't jerk it from my hand without first dislocating my shoulder. Which may well have been a possibility. It was then that I got my first clear indication of how well-trained the dog was. He walked with me to Patty, sat down, and gazed patiently up at her as she scratched his head and told him how handsome he was.

"I was there when they brought him in for treatment. He was one unhappy pup that day, let me tell you. And I was there when the family came in with news that he was lost. God..." She shook her head. "I don't know who needed a tranquilizer most, the parents or the kids."

"I can't even imagine," I said. "That's got to be a horrible feeling."

She paused for a moment, then looked up at me and said, "It is."

Two words reflecting painful experience. You could see it in her eyes, but I refrained from asking.

Patty led the two of us over to the split rail fence, stopping a couple of yards short of it. Her dogs could have come through that token decorative barrier, but stood wagging and making eager sounds instead. I pointed that out.

"We believe in training," she replied. "That fence is as far as they're allowed without permission and they know it." She made a gesture with her hand and both dogs wiggled under the lowest rail and stood behind her, sweeping dust into the warm late afternoon air with vigorous tails. Toby came up on all four and made a sound I hoped meant he was happy.

She allowed them to close the gap; I tightened my grip on the leash. Dog noses touched. Dog bodies quivered. There was circling and sniffing of both ends of dogs, as dogs do. It was quickly obvious there would be no animosity, something underlined in bold when the dog Percy darted back into his yard, raced to one of the shrubby junipers decorating the yard, and raced back with a heavy-duty tug-o-war dog toy, which was dropped on the ground in front of Toby.

"Yeah, we're good," said Patty, retrieving the toy. "Come on in."

Through the gate and into the yard, with the resident pups trotting briskly along, around the house and into the properly fenced backyard. We stayed on hand to supervise, but took Toby off the leash. All three dogs raced off, running and barking, tussling and generally raising dust. We chatted and watched until they'd burned off more energy than I've had since I was sixteen years old, at which point water was provided and slopped everywhere. Patty issued instructions, and three bowls of food were brought out by her boys and set a fair distance apart. The food vanished into the three dogs quickly and without so much as a grumble of complaint.

"That's one hell of a dog you have there," Patty said. "His owners made sure he was properly socialized."

"It's refreshing," I said. "I've known far too many dogs that wouldn't even come when their owners called them."

"Proper training is the only way to go, in my opinion, regardless of breed." She waved a hand toward the patio furniture, and we sat on opposite sides of a long, wooden table. "Essential, with this breed, even if Frank is right and this one isn't one hundred percent."

"Are they really that much trouble?" I asked.

She shook her head and said, "Not by their inclination, at least, not in my somewhat limited experience. But they are smarter than the average breed, a damned sight stronger, and courageous to a fault. Also damned stubborn when they feel the need. That's bad news in an undisciplined animal. A disaster waiting to happen in one that's been abused, a situation that accounts for most of the lurid headlines, I think. Well-meaning folk rescue one of these, have no idea what they have on the leash, and something really bad happens."

The three dogs were in the middle of the yard by then, investigating the small pond there that mercifully no one had yet jumped into. The pair of white ducks on the pond looked anxious.

"I don't get the sense that Toby has anything like a mean streak in him."

"He doesn't," Patty replied. "I've known enough dogs to see that. Still, I wouldn't cross him for any money. There's a lot of strength there. Piss that dog off, and you don't walk away in one piece. Assuming you could still walk."

"What you said about courage." And I told her about the bear.

Patty's eyes widened. "That was a close call. Damned close! And more proof that Toby is smarter even than the average pittie. He read that the same way you did. The bear just wanted to pass through. You did that exactly right. And he stayed between you and the bear the whole time?"

"In a direct line between us. Like you said, courageous and perhaps loyal to a fault."

"Huh..." She looked from me to the dogs and back. "Attached himself to you quickly, too. Well, it's often said that dogs just know when a person is right. Lot of people tried to catch or lure him, according to Laurel, and yet you managed to snag him."

"I wouldn't say 'snagged' exactly. He came to me. All I did was talk to him. I was going to set out some food for him, the way other campers had been doing, and when I turned from the stove there he was. Your ranger friend, Laurel, took advantage of that. I saw it as a huge imposition, at first, but the big guy really knows how to get under your skin."

"Frank said you were thinking of driving Toby home," she said.

"Not thinking," I replied. "That's the plan, unless his owners say otherwise. We're supposed to hash that out this evening."

"Incredibly generous of you."

I shrugged and said, "I really was headed that way, eventually. Didn't exactly have a timetable. This little mission just injects a bit of purpose into things."

"On the road for the sake of traveling?"

"Something like that," I replied. I didn't elaborate, and though she gave a look that said there were guesses and questions, she didn't pry.

We sat in companionable silence for a while, shaded by the porch, but feeling the warmth of the day. Iced tea was brought out by her daughter, the oldest of the three kids. She struck me as a bit on the shy side, and already very attractive, with a strong resemblance to her mother. Blushed easily, to judge by her reaction to my thanks for the refreshment.

"Great kids," I said.

"Thanks," Patty replied. "A little harder to train than the dogs, but I think we've managed."

She sounded me out on matters to do with food, making sure I suffered from no food allergies or restrictions based on politics or personal beliefs. About then the good doctor finally turned up, later than he'd intended due to a conversation with the Sheriff on the way out. I was shown to the guest house on the property so I could clean up for dinner. I needed it, those cold showers being brief and less than effective. Clothes that needed laundering were confiscated, with the promise that all would be returned when clean. I started to feel like I was being adopted. For sure, they all treated me like visiting family. I was out of the shower and feeling refreshed, with my last clean shirt and pair of jeans on, when I realized I heard children laughing and dogs barking. Stepping to the door of the small guest house I saw that a blue plastic wading pool had been set out and filled with water. And not just any water; there were rafts and clouds of soap suds all over the immediate surroundings. In the middle of the mess were three very wet and soapy dogs, and two shirtless boys of a similar condition.

Frank stood by with a garden hose, which he wielded with obvious experience. Looking to where I stood, he smiled and waved. Raising his voice so it could be heard over the soapy bedlam between us, he said, "Thought the dogs could use a bit of freshening. Same with the boys."

"Efficient," I replied, laughing as Toby bounced out of the pool and then back in with a tremendous splash that prompted barking and laughter. He looked my way, a tall hat of foam on his head. Toby shook, and the foam wadded up and splashed straight into Pete's face. Outrage was expressed and hilarity ensued.

*

"You were in good hands," Sam said.

"Tell me about it," I replied. "I was sorry at the time that I could only stay for such a short time. But I stopped and spent a few days with them on the way home. Apparently, I'm welcome any time."

"That's a wonderful thing to know, isn't it?"

"Yes, it certainly is."

*

The cooking had been done while I was cleaning up, and the air around the house was fragrant in that way that kicks an appetite into high gear. Not that I needed much encouragement, having last eaten early that morning. Frank and I had a few minutes at the big wooden table before food was brought out, and I confessed to the mention of guns being drawn.

Frank wore a rueful grin as he shook his head. "I heard about that. Don't worry, I'd have given her the full account tonight. And in a town this small, it wouldn't have been a secret more than overnight anyway."

I was left on my own for a few minutes as he went inside to help with final preparations. The dinner that followed was a feast of salad, fresh bread, grilled chicken, and sliced cucumbers that came from the garden on one side of the back yard. Simple food but good and plentiful, served out of doors at that big wooden table. We'd just finished and sent the kids off to do other things, and were in the comfortable and slightly care-worn family room with a scatter of drowsy dogs and that delayed adult beverage, when the call came from the Vernons. Frank took it and after a few moments announced that the matter would be handled via computers and webcams, rather than a conference call. Patty and I followed him into his home office; the dogs gradually trailed along, with Toby bringing up the rear.

The Vernon family was packed together in an attempt to get everyone into view on Frank's computer screen, which Frank twisted around to face into the room. Their effort wasn't entirely successful, and it was a while before I was sure that there were four Vernon offspring present — two girls and two boys. Mrs. Vernon was an attractive woman with short dark brown hair. Mr. Vernon appeared older than his wife, with lighter brown hair graying at the temples. Everyone looked bleary from tears that may have come from remembered loss or sudden hope, or both. The youngest boy was sniffling, and big sister, the oldest of the quartet, sat with an arm around his skinny shoulders. All four of them had hair as dark as Mom's. Mr. Vernon did most of the talking and, after Frank made the introductions, I gave most of the answers.

But first, we walked Toby into the middle of the room and put the camera on him. He seemed puzzled by what was going on, and the voices of his family coming through small computer speakers brought no sign of recognition. Still, they all knew their dog when they saw him, and proclaimed this by shouting his name and emitting other variously happy noises. Concern was expressed over how thin he was, and his inflamed eye and the cat claw marks did not escape notice. Frank assured him that all these matters were being addressed. Their eyes were a little redder around the edges before the real conversation began, on both ends of the connection.

"It's all a bit overwhelming," Mr. Vernon said when their curiosities had been satisfied.

"We'd given up hope — and now this. Mr. Ford, I honestly don't know what to say to your offer..."

"I generally go by my first name," I said.

"Fair enough," he replied. "I'm Jim, my wife is Elaine, and from oldest to youngest we have Sarah, Martin, Elizabeth, and William."

"Billy!" the youngest one corrected in no uncertain terms. Sarah laughed and ruffled his hair with her free hand.

"Well, as I said to Elaine this afternoon, I'm headed your way. This extended vacation I'm on has no real game plan, and I wasn't planning on dawdling on my way across the middle of the country. People I know and want to visit are in the Chicago area and points well north of there."

"I get what you're saying," Jim admitted. "But he's our dog and, well..."

"You see him as your responsibility," Frank finished.

"Exactly that," Jim replied, looking and sounding chagrined. "I mean, we let him get lost in the first place."

"That's not the way I heard it," I said. "But in any case, accidents happen to even the most careful folks. So, let's just be practical here. How long do you think it would take you to get here and pick Toby up from Dr. Nelson? Assuming, of course, he and his family were okay with hosting Toby in the meantime."

"Which we would be," Patty assured us.

"Gawd, I don't know," Jim said, a worried frown on what I took to be an otherwise good-natured face. "We pretty much shot whatever vacation time either of us had extending that last trip, trying to find Toby. I'd need to talk to my employer. Same for Elaine."

"We could work something out," Elaine put in. "I'm sure we could."

"So, let's assume your respective employers are willing to let you drop everything and run out here," I said. "Flying or driving?"

"Driving." Jim didn't even hesitate. "I've seen way too many news stories lately. I wouldn't trust Toby to any airline."

"So, even if you really push things along, you're probably looking at a ten-day round trip," I said. "Assuming no problems along the way."

"To say nothing of preparing for the trip," Jim muttered. "A day or two to get permissions, another day — at least — to have the van checked out for a long drive." He'd gone from frowning to glowering in frustration.

"Would the kids be coming along?" Frank asked.

"Ah, no," said Elaine. Her next words were drowned out by angry denials from the aforementioned children. She made stern noises at them and they subsided quickly, with expressions that mirrored their worried father. "Their schools are on the quarter system," she explained. "They won't be available for a road trip for a month." That was followed by more grumbled protests, albeit quieter ones.

"So," I continued. "A week to ten days, at least. If I start tomorrow morning, I should have him home in less than half that time."

"Well, as Patty has said, if you don't want to do it this way, Toby is welcome here until you can arrange things," Frank said. "If you need the night to think it over..."

"Do you trust him, Dr. Nelson?" Elaine asked. "Do you trust Mr. Ford?"

Frank glanced at me, then faced the webcam. "Yes," he said. "I do."

"More to the point," Patty added, "Toby trusts him. There's already a very strong bond between them. Toby's made his decision, from what I see, and I know when to trust a dog. I do believe they'll be able to travel together. Paul will get Toby home to you, all other things being equal."

I must admit it was a serious feel-good moment, complete with a lump in my throat, hearing that from people who barely knew me. Something of my reaction must have shown, because both of the Nelsons grinned at me. Toby chose that moment to get up, amble over to me, and rest his wide chin on my knee while wagging his tail. I put my hand on his head, and the wag sped went up.

"Toby only does that with people he really likes," said Billy. "Toby trusts that man."

"Between kids and dog... All right," said Jim with a glance at Elaine, who merely nodded her agreement. "That's the plan, then. And damned if I know how to thank you enough!"

"I think you just did, Jim," I replied. "By entrusting me with such an important errand.

That means a lot to me."

"Could we trouble you to stay in touch on the road?" Elaine asked. The suggestion was followed by nods and sounds of agreement from her family.

Before I could respond, their oldest, Sarah, spoke up. "He could use the blog!" When her parents both turned toward her she continued, sounding a little defensive. "I could set it so Paul — uh, I mean, Mr. Ford — can post to it. He could do that whenever he could get Wi-Fi. Which is just about anywhere, these days."

"I thought we took that weblog down?" her father asked. Before she could respond, Jim laughed quietly and said, "That's okay, sweetie. I suppose none of us really gave up hope. Not completely."

In moments I had the weblog and physical addresses I needed, along with a couple of phone numbers, and made a promise to check out the blog that evening. I also promised to be on the road the next morning, an early start for my mission to take Toby back where he belonged. When I pulled my laptop out of the bag, back in the quiet, softly lit guest house, I found that young Sarah had already added me to the site. I logged on and posted in a nutshell the tale of how Toby and I had gotten together. The version that was safe to tell, I mean. I shared the adventure with the bear, but said nothing of events earlier that day in town. I closed the post with the announcement that Toby's journey home would begin the next day.

It never occurred to me to see how many

followers that blog had, and so I was stunned and amazed to see that the post, the following morning, had garnered more than a thousand "likes," and a couple hundred posts in response.

"Toby," I said as the first light of day came through the window. "I had no idea I was hanging with a celebrity."

Toby just whuffled a bit and rested his chin on my leg as I sat there.

« 6 »

The first day of our trip started with an enormous breakfast for both man and beast. Toby and his two buds bedeviled the ducks in the pond for a while — the ducks expressed their annoyance loudly, but were unharmed — ate generous portions, and waited patiently for tidbits as the two-legged folk feasted on pancakes, eggs, bacon, and melon on the back patio yet again. When the weather was fine, I was told, the Nelsons rarely ate indoors. And this morning was as fine as they come, with a clear blue sky and only a trace of breeze bearing the scent of pine trees; cool and quiet with the world around us at peace. The food was excellent, and the coffee first-rate. A laptop was brought out and the Bring Toby Home weblog was examined. Some questionable posts I'd noticed at sunrise, admonishing profanely against trusting the dog to a stranger, were gone. I'd flagged them for Sarah when I spotted the trolls, with an offer to deal with such nonsense directly in the future.

"I've got this," was her response. After that it was never necessary for me to step in and back the kid up. She responded when she needed to, without flinching. Repeat offenders were generally blocked without comment and, apparently, without remorse. When she felt a need to respond, the words she posted were calm, clever, and frequently humorous — often at the offender's expense. A number of those who received such a response tipped their cap to her, apologized, and went on to post more politely in the future. I found myself looking forward to meeting Sarah.

The time came for goodbyes, and as I was shaking Frank's hand and promising to visit on my return journey, he said, "Stop by the general store on your way out of town. They have some stuff there ready for you to pick up."

"Stuff?"

"Basic dog supplies," he replied with a smile. "Food, bowls, spare harnesses and leads. Definitely ditch that collar and go with a harness."

"Come on, you didn't need to do that," I said, more than a little embarrassed. "I was going to stop on the way out and get whatever was needed."

"We didn't do it," Patty said. "The Vernon family called it in."

"Ah, well then."

"Just taking care of their dog," Frank explained.

"Of course they are." I opened the rear passenger side door and turned to call Toby, but he was already trotting along and a moment later was sitting upright on the back seat, tongue hanging out, looking around as if absolutely everything deserved his attention. I was grateful at that point that Patty had volunteered to trim his nails, thereby preventing worse damage to seat covers than Toby had done the day before. "Looks like someone is more than ready to hit the road."

"I could swear he knows what's going on," Frank said.

"That wouldn't surprise me one bit," I replied.

One last round of farewells, and I was behind the wheel, taking it slow on the graded dirt road to avoid dusting the laundry I saw hanging from their widely scattered neighbors' clothes lines. We turned onto the paved county road and made better speed, and soon were back in town. The rustic general store — seriously, it was made of logs — was already well known to me; I'd come in often enough for supplies that my face was recognized. The owner waved at me from behind the counter, then came around to greet Toby, who he seemed to know all about.

"Those folks in Illinois gotta be beside themselves," he said. "Knowing they're gettin' the big fella back."

"They bought a bunch of stuff for him, I'm

told."

"That they did," he said. He was a portly fellow, middle-aged with thin, pale hair, and less than flexible. He always ended up short of breath if the place was busy and he had to hustle from one customer to another. "Hey, Ricky! Bring that box up front for me. The bag of dog food, too." There was a muffled response; a moment later a sandy-haired teenaged boy appeared with a cardboard box tucked under one arm and a large bag of dog chow slung over his shoulder. Ricky looked like someone who enjoyed spending time in a gym, though how he managed that in a town lacking such a facility, I could only imagine. He set the box on the counter as if it weighed next to nothing.

"That's yours?" he asked, pointing to my SUV outside the store. When I said it was and that it was unlocked, he strode out the front door and put the dog food in the back with my gear. Returning to the store, he held his hand down to be smelled by Toby, and when the hand was accepted with a lick, proceeded to thoroughly scratch Toby's head and neck. "Whole town's talking about you guys. That must have been something, seeing those dudes hauled away."

"I could have skipped that part," I admitted. "Standing in that office with people who were ready and willing to shoot wasn't my idea of a fun time. Fortunately, that FBI agent was on top of it. Bad guys didn't know who she was until too late."

"Yeah, I saw her talking to Sheriff Schofield yesterday afternoon." He grinned. "Serious hotness!"

His boss rolled his eyes. "You have work to do. Git!" Without responding, Ricky sauntered off. "Kid's got more hormones than brains."

"Didn't we all, at that age?"

"Hell, I can't remember that far back." He laughed at that, and then we inventoried the contents of the box. It was all as Frank had said, except for the yellow, heavy-duty dog toy that bore a striking resemblance to one of those animated Japanese critters everyone runs around stalking with cell phones.

"What's this?"

"Dog toy," he explained. "My wife's idea." He gave me a wink and added, "On the house!"

I carried the box out and tucked it in back with everything else, then took a moment to replace the collar with a harness, as Frank had suggested. The storekeeper came out with me, squinting a bit in the bright morning sunshine.

"Thank you, sir," I said. I handed the toy to Toby, who seemed to know exactly what it was for. He gave it a shake, as if testing it, then jumped up into the back seat once more.

"Bet that thing lasts a day," the storekeeper said.

"It'll be a fun day for someone, then."

"Well, sir, it's a fine thing you're doing," he said, shaking my hand. "Honored to be a little part of it. Safe trip, and if you ever pass through here again, stop by and tell me all about it."

"I intend to," I replied. "Dr. Nelson's family is leaving a light on for me."

"Fine people," he said with a nod.

"You into the whole internet, social media thing?" I asked.

"Some," he said. "My wife is more into that sort of thing than I am. Keeps in touch with family using it."

I gave him the name of the weblog. "I'll be posting progress reports for the Vernons and Toby's fans. You can follow us real-time."

"You know, I just might do that."

"I'll drop by anyway, though." Which pleased him.

*

"And did you stop on the way home?" Sam asked.

Nodding, I said, "Spent several days there with the Nelsons. Got a hero's welcome from the town."

"Well, considering what happened along the way, that isn't too surprising."

"I suppose not," I said. "But that's getting ahead of the story."

*

I was briefly tempted to drive back up to the campground and thank Laurel for her help, but if the camp hosts were still there, I might have done something regrettable if I ran into them. So, I headed out south and east, as straight as possible. Which wasn't very straight for a while. Eventually made it to Santa Fe and from there to Interstate 40. After that it was cruise control, lots of music, and a dog that seemed immune to boredom. Toby drowsed from time to time, but when he wasn't asleep, he was watching the world roll by outside the windows. A great appreciator of landscapes, even those without much in the way of features, or so it would seem. Who knows what a dog sees out the window of a moving vehicle? He seemed completely relaxed and was undemanding until he needed to make a stop. I correctly guessed what brought on the whining the first time, and was spared an unpleasant and messy lesson learned the hard way.

The time it took to reach the interstate was longer than I might have expected. I didn't know the territory, having come into the area by following a different route. I'd gone north through eastern Arizona, east through the Navajo Reservation, then east across New Mexico through Farmington. So even with modern navigational aids I was in unfamiliar territory and managed to make a wrong turn that wasn't obvious soon enough. It took more than five hours to make it to Amarillo, and since we hadn't come even close to leaving at the break of day — more like mid-morning — that's as far as I wanted to push it. When I realized we'd be stopping in Amarillo for the night, I pulled over at a rest stop, let Toby do his thing — which included making friends and influencing people — and then used my phone to find a place to stay that was pet friendly. I made a reservation and drove on.

The mountains and forests were quickly behind us, and we drove through wide open land that wasn't quite flat, over which towering thunderstorms were rising. Watching the storms build up and grow ever darker, I wondered how Toby might handle thunder and lightning. I've known dogs who were reduced to quivering lumps of terror at the sound of firecrackers. Lightning and thunder? I made a mental note to ask Sarah about this when I checked in with the Vernon web guru that evening. Even as I had that thought, a storm to the southwest, very dark and flat underneath, stabbed the grasslands with a bright fork of lightning. In time, a low grumble of thunder rolled out to us. It seemed I would have the answer to that question long before logging on.

Toby glanced out the window on that side, then resumed his normal eyes-front perusal of the road ahead as if nothing had happened. Of course, that storm was many miles away, and anything but a fair test.

My thoughts wandered as I drove through a land that was quickly darkened by the shadows of clouds, becoming a patchwork of green and dark gray. I'd hit the road in an effort to re-orient myself and clear my head after the train wreck my life had become. And I'd gone from an FBI investigation that wrecked the train to an FBI agent aiming a gun at a couple of bad guys. What kind of luck puts two things like that in the path of one life? My mind was boggled. Those thoughts eventually turned to the fate Toby had somehow escaped. Other dogs weren't so fortunate. It made me want to hit someone, and not just anyone. Fortunately, the culprits were in custody and a long way behind us, so the chance to possibly get myself killed by doing something really stupid was greatly reduced.

*

Looking around and making sure we were on our own, Sam asked, "Whatever became of those two? Or their bosses?"

"An FBI agent contacted me and took a statement, pretty much the story I just told you. I was never called to testify, and no defense attorneys bothered to check in with me, but I followed the trial. The two dudes were given stiff sentences, even after copping pleas at the expense of their employers. The family paying them fared worse. The matriarch and her husband were both convicted of murder and conspiracy, among other things, and received life sentences."

"So, no one is likely to come after you? That's got to be a relief."

"I suppose so," I replied. "Never gave it that much thought. My impression was that my statement was used more to evaluate the Special Agent's work than for anything else.

Doubtful those people ever knew my name."

"And that camp host?" Sam asked.

"Ah, yes! The camp hosts. He and his wife pulled up stakes and took off the same day I took Toby down the road to see the good doctor. When I passed through town on the way home, no one had any clue where the bastards were or what became of them. If they're smart they'll stay hell and gone away from that place. One of the dogs that disappeared belonged to Sheriff Schofield's niece."

"Oh, dear!"

"Yep. My impression of that lawman was that the Wild West was alive and well in his person. If he or one of his deputies catches them, it won't go easy for that pair."

"Well, I hope they do catch them!"

"Me, too."

*

If you like wide open spaces, horizon to horizon, that stretch of I-40, from where highway 285 crosses I-40, all the way to Amarillo, is what you're looking for. The only other time I've been through there, on my return trip, there were times when I could swear I wasn't moving forward at all. I could see the roadside streaming past me, but looking ahead and behind, the view never seemed to change. It's kind of a creepy illusion for someone accustomed to hills and mountains and a coastline. I couldn't cross the area fast enough. It's even flatter for a while east of Amarillo. Every now and then a small cluster of buildings flashed by, some of them clearly deserted. Occasionally there was an agricultural facility with silos, barns, and sheds. These looked too industrial to me to be called farms. I think it was the lack of anything resembling a house in sight that made me feel that way. We passed a set of long, low buildings that were almost shockingly white, even in that early twilight you get when the sunlight is filtered by storm clouds. From the smell we drove through, pretty sure they were full of chickens.

The long stands of windmills, those big white ones with long, slim blades that generate electricity, were eye-catching in that setting, and something of a relief when they rose out of the broad green fields flanking the highway. The sight of a grove of trees almost came as something of a shock when one appeared. It might have been a dull, almost mind-numbing view, had it not been for the weather. That afternoon, and into the early evening, the storms around us grew together and congealed, darkening as they crowded in on us. It felt like the storms were drawing together in a ragged black line and herding us eastward. We were staying ahead of the front that was surely driving things, but at the rate that new storms were appearing and growing along the leading edge, staying ahead of the weather seemed ever less likely. I wouldn't be wasting any time getting into the hotel, when we got there, that was certain.

Amarillo just suddenly seems to be there. You're driving through green, flat land, some of it clearly farmland, with a scatter of buildings and highway signs, and then just like that you're in the town. Or so it seemed to someone accustomed to life here in the Bay Area. Maybe it was an illusion, but it really seemed abrupt to me. It was a quiet weekday evening when I rolled in, but the town didn't impress me as "sleepy" in that way towns in the West are so often portrayed. The hotel was on the west side of town, just off the freeway, and looked like it had been built in the early Sixties. It was, however, immaculate, nicely landscaped with tall trees and flowering shrubs, and clearly prosperous, as was the busy diner between the hotel and the freeway. Two single-story wings flanked the central lobby. Vehicles were pulling into the parking lot from the road, their operators no doubt seeking shelter rather than driving on through a night of storms. The light was failing quickly as rising clouds blotted out the late afternoon sun. Night would come early. The wind was picking up and smelled of rain. I was glad I'd called ahead and made a reservation.

Thunder rumbled behind me as I got out and told Toby that I would be right back. He peered at me, that lumpy yellow dog toy clutched in his jaws, and gave a nervous whine. It occurred to me that, since we'd met, I'd never really been out of his sight.

"Hey, buddy, it's okay," I said. "I'll just be a few minutes." The whining became more frantic. I sighed and got the heavy leash from the box of supplies and clipped it to his harness. "What the hell? They say they're pet friendly."

Toby dropped the toy on the back seat, hopped down, and trotted along beside me. An elderly man paused to hold the door for us as he headed back outside.

"Thanks," I said.

"He's a big one," the man observed.

"That he is."

"Pit bull?"

"Mostly, from what I'm told. He clearly has mixed parentage."

"My brother has a couple," he said. "Raised 'em from pups and did it right, so they behave real well. But they ain't anywhere near this tall!" All the while letting Toby thoroughly inspect his hand. He clearly passed muster in Toby's view. Of course, by then I was aware that Toby gave everyone he met, people and dogs, more than half a chance.

A loud boom of thunder rolled across the land, and Toby flinched. I got us inside and ignored the double-takes of the four people waiting in line who glanced our way. When you're escorted into the building by a dog as sturdy as Toby, people take notice. Some of them, when they think they recognize the breed, either look wary, or try to pretend you're not there. The woman ahead of me in line, holding the leash to a small, shaggy dog of uncertain pedigree, did neither. She smiled and said, "He's a handsome fellow. What's his name?"

"Toby."

"Good choice. It suits him." She glanced down at her dog, who was quivering with his eagerness to make Toby's acquaintance, and said, "Mind your manners, Kermie."

"Not my dog, actually, so I didn't name him," I said. "But you're right, it does suit him."

"Not yours?"

"His real family lost him," I explained, not wanting to go into details. "I'm giving him a lift home."

"That's so kind of you." She looked down quickly as if to admonish Kermie again, then laughed and said, "Seems they've worked it out. I do hope Toby is up to date."

"Up to date?"

"Vaccinations."

"Ah, yes, he is, as a matter of fact." I was pretty sure a family that worried about a lost dog that much would have given him at least basic medical care. And it did turn out that I wasn't fibbing.

The two dogs were nose to nose, whuffling and wagging, obviously delighted to meet each other. That Toby was easily several times Kermie's size seemed to matter not in the slightest. I don't believe dogs see breeds the way we do, so Toby's friendly body language just translated as Bigger Dog Being Nice To Me to Kermie, who was clearly a well-socialized animal. We patted our respective canines and told them they were good boys, and then Kermie's owner — short and blond and dressed as if on a business trip, dog notwithstanding — signed in and wished us a pleasant night. A bright flash and a loud bang rattled the world outside. Toby flinched violently and stared back the way we'd come.

Kermie let out a bark, and Toby turned toward the other dog, who wagged vigorously. As the woman holding Kermie's leash chuckled, I said, "I think that was dog for 'Dude, don't freak, it's just the weather!'"

"You may be right." And went off down the hall to find her room.

It was my turn. I identified myself, and the tired-looking man behind the desk — his name badge identified him as George Willis, Manager — tapped away at his keyboard.

"Ah, here you are, Mr. Ford. One single occupancy." He leaned forward and looked down at Toby, who looked up and wagged. "Though if *you* were much bigger, I'd have to call it double."

"Toby, my boy, next time someone tells you size doesn't matter, pee on his leg," I said. The clerk and the half dozen people now behind me laughed.

"You'll find signs at the exits pointing to the dog yard," Mr. Willis said. "We try to keep it clean, but your assistance would be appreciated. There's a dispenser with bags on a post, for your convenience." Another flash of lightning and a louder rumble. The storms were very near. "With any luck, it'll still be there in the morning."

"I came well supplied, as a matter of fact," I assured him. "I haven't seen a weather report lately. How rough a night are we in for?"

"There was a tornado watch issued just before we pulled off the highway," said a man's voice behind me. "So, it has potential. All the wrong sort of potential."

I took my key — which these days is more like a credit card than a traditional key — and stepped out of the line. Behind me stood a young African-American couple and a small boy who couldn't have been more than five or six years old; the father had been the one with the weather report. The boy's eyes were wide, his face pinched by anxiety. "Not exactly what anyone wanted to hear tonight," I said. "Especially this fellow, I'm guessing."

"No, Kyle is definitely not a a fan of thunderstorms," said the mother.

"Neither is Toby, here," I said, reaching down to pat the dog's shoulder. "Well, maybe this will all blow over quickly."

"That would be nice," said Kyle's father. "Not counting on it, though."

I led Toby out into a breezy evening that smelled of rain and ozone. The wind was getting frisky. Toby stayed in contact with my leg, shoulder to knee, looking nervous. I pulled out our overnight bags — one for me and one for the dog, prepped at the stop where I phoned in our reservation. Toby snagged the dog toy from the back seat. It must have been like holding a security blanket, because with the next rumble of thunder he looked around nervously, but kept his pace casual as we reentered the lobby and headed for the hallway that would lead us to our room.

The family I'd met in the lobby was on their way down the same hall, the mother trying to juggle two small bags while holding the boy's hand. Her husband was dragging a bulky suitcase along, the kind with the little wheels and the extendable handle. Kyle was pale and clearly unhappy, which was no wonder, with the wind beginning to howl outside. As if searching for a diversion, he looked back when he saw us following along, then stopped and said, "Can I pet him?"

His parents stopped and turned. "His family includes a kid about this one's age," I assured them. "And this big fellow is about as people-oriented as any dog I've ever known."

"Oh, why not?" said the father. The mother gave him a look that clearly meant she thought he was crazy, but she said nothing.

Kyle approached and I felt Toby's weight shift toward the boy. That tail started to wag, whacking my left knee with a clearly audible and almost painful thump. The whine Toby emitted was an eager, happy sound. Kyle's father reminded him of how he had been shown to pet a grandparent's dog, and Kyle very carefully held one hand out for Toby to sniff. Which Toby did, following the gesture with a lick. The kid came to stand beside Toby and patted his shoulder.

The storm chose that moment to unleash

its full fury, in a sequence of lightning flashes and sharp concussions, with a gust of wind that rattled doors and windows all through the structure. The hotel lights flickered twice, and then mercifully stayed on. Toby and Kyle both flinched and let out the pitiful sounds of a frightened dog and badly startled boy. Kyle, before any of us could react, threw his arms around Toby's neck. "It's okay, Toby," he said. "It's okay."

*

"Many dogs react very badly to that sort of sudden contact," said Sam.

"That's for sure," the store manager added. He had come to stand at the end of the table, obviously curious about what I was up to. I'd given him a nod when he arrived; he raised no objections. "Had some bad things happen here because someone's kid crowded a strange dog."

"It scared the hell out me, quite frankly," I said. "His mother was definitely not happy about it. But Toby made us all feel more than a little foolish a heartbeat later."

*

Toby turned toward Kyle, put his chin across the boy's shoulder, and tucked that skinny little kid body up against a broad, brown dog chest. The lumpy dog toy dangled between the kid's shoulder blades. He was sitting back on his haunches and that bullwhip tail was sweeping a blurred arc across the carpeting. The mother made one of those noises mothers make when something is just too cute to bear. Whatever fear the size of the dog might have inspired was gone in a heartbeat.

We let them stand that way until the main squall line's open salvo had faded. "Okay, Kyle, time to get to our room," said his father.

"But Toby is still scared," he protested, his wide eyes making it plain the dog wasn't the only one.

"He certainly was," I said. "But he's okay now, thanks to you."

Clearly reluctant, Kyle stepped away from the dog and patted him on the shoulder. "Okay," he said, sounding very uncertain, and look his mother's offered hand.

Toby was shivering and pressing himself against my leg again. "Funny thing," I said then to Kyle's father, as I tried to comfort the dog. "He stood his ground with a bear. A big one, too."

Thunder shook the world again.

"That's a lot bigger than a bear," the father said with an upward glance. He patted Toby on the head, told him he was a good dog, and followed his wife and son.

« 7 »

I had just enough time online to get some feedback from the Vernon web guru before the lights went out.

After all was said and done, I learned that the line of storms had not simply crossed the town from west to east, but on more of a diagonal path, southwest to northeast. Instead of a wave of storms rolling over us, there and done, the entire damned system crawled over us, one end to the other, with storm centers apparently gaining in strength all the while.

*

Sam was frowning at me as she tried to picture what I was saying. I took the ballpoint pen on the table between us and put a small circle on a scrap of paper. "This is Amarillo," I said. "The pen is the storm front. I thought it was going this way," and simply swept the barrel of the pen over the circle. "But it did this." I dragged the pen at a shallow angle so that the length of the pen gradually crossed over the circle, with just enough sideways motion for the circle to go from one side of the pen to the other.

She nodded and said, "Got it."

*

However, by the time we'd settled in the room, I'd managed to convince myself that the worst of the storm was over. But while I was speaking via internet to Sarah Vernon, the storm made me a liar in a big way, increasing its intensity with alarming suddenness. She could actually hear the thunder over the laptop's built-in microphone — the rumble and roar had become pretty much continuous — and finally said, "Look, this isn't safe. If you have a strike nearby while plugged into that laptop..."

"Was just thinking of that," I admitted.

"Toby staying calm?"

"So far," I replied. "He'd rather this weather was happening to someone else, but seems okay so long as I'm cool with things."

"He's like that," she said. "Really good at reading people. Also means he trusts you."

"That's good to know."

"Well, I'm signing off, Mr. Ford. Don't worry about the trolls. I'll deal with them."

"I have no doubts about that. Good night, Sarah. I'll check in again tomorrow."

She logged off and I shut down the laptop, sliding it into a compartment of my overnight bag. The wind was howling in a way that made me suddenly uneasy, though at first I didn't know why. I noticed that Toby was standing up, alert in that way he had displayed with the bear in the campground. "You okay, there?" I asked. He looked up at me and gave a nervous whine. His tail drooped, then tucked down between his legs.

I walked over and put my hand on his head and realized that Toby was shaking like a leaf. In that same moment, a low grinding roar finally registered on me, and in that same moment, the roaring went from a background noise to something more like a wall of sound. Had the man said something about a tornado watch? It had just become a warning, so far as I was concerned. Something bigger than a bear. A hell of a lot bigger. I'd never been in a tornado before, but I'd read enough about them that I could guess what was out there, and had the sense to get us away from the hotel room window. The lights flickered as the power cut in and out. "Damn! Toby, come!"

Three long strides took me into the small bathroom. There was a shower stall; not a tub, but it would have to do. "Here!" I shouted over the noise, but Toby needed no encouragement. He sprinted into the bathroom with me and I slammed the door shut, locking it. Grabbing his harness, I marched him into the shower and dragged the curtain shut. No idea why I thought that mattered. We hunkered down together, Toby crowding me and whining, shaking badly. I put my arms around him and held on. At that moment the power failed outright, and we were plunged into a surreal darkness punctuated by flashes of brilliant white light coming through the tiny bathroom window. The noise was insane, the grinding, howling roar mixed with the sound of impacts against the wall and shattering glass.

I'm a California boy, and have been in some earthquakes, including the Loma Prieta quake in 1989. This was worse. Somehow, it felt more personal, as if the tornado had singled us out for destruction. Perhaps not the most rational reaction, but who can be rational while enduring the wrath of the elements? Something was out there, something beyond any power of mine to fend off; a discrete something, with a focus an earthquake lacks. Not a comfortable feeling, knowing that this thing was just beyond the hotel wall, tearing up the little corner of the world that happened to include me. I think I experienced fear in its purest form that night.

I held the dog as tight as I could, my back to the thin door between us and the forces battering the hotel. My ears popped as if the air pressure had just dropped. At the same time the sound of storm became overwhelming, a physical force beyond mere noise. Toby cried out in a high-pitched sound of fear that I could barely hear over the roaring and pounding. One flash of lightning burned an image of his face into my mind, of teeth bared in terror and eyes white almost all the way around. If that dog had panicked, there wouldn't have been a thing I could have done to restrain him. But Toby just sat there, trembling; he knew this was not a thing you could run from, and he trusted me to keep him safe, but he was still frightened half to death.

That made two of us.

And just like that the noise level dropped to the sound of strong wind blowing. The lightning and thunder continued, but by themselves they seemed quieter, almost muted. That was the weirdest part of the whole thing, the way it ended. It was just done, replaced by ordinary wind and the sound of heavy rain, and those, too, faded away in just a few minutes. It grew quiet enough that I could hear people shouting outside in the darkness. Standing up, I felt a cold, wet breeze swirl around me. By a flicker of lightning, I found the source; the bathroom window was gone, apparently sucked out of its frame without a trace remaining.

I waited until the frequency of lightning flashes diminished and the thunder sounded further off, and only then opened the bathroom door. Toby stood up but made no effort to follow me. That suited me, since I knew I'd heard glass shattering, and the last thing I needed just then was a dog with bloody paws. The carpet was soggy under my feet, but I was relieved to hear nothing like broken glass crunching. I groped my way to the bed, which was now at an angle to the wall, telling Toby to stay when I heard him whine. The only light coming in was from a flickering emergency lamp hanging in the hallway, shining through the now open door to the room. Water streamed through a gaping hole in the ceiling. It took me a moment to realize the door was flat on the floor. By some miracle my bag was still on the bed; Toby's was on the floor nearby, pretty much where I'd left it. There was a small but powerful flashlight in my bag, and I fished it out to have a look around.

Toby was sitting in the doorway to the bathroom where I'd left him, head down and shivering. I examined the floor and saw no broken glass, even though the window and the curtains were gone. Leaning over the window sill with the light, I realized the storm had also sucked this window out rather than blowing it in. Counting my blessings, I called Toby to me, pretty sure by that point it was safe for his feet. Toby started toward me, glanced to one side and lunged. Before I had time to wonder what was going on, he trotted to me with that lumpy dog toy in his mouth.

"Love your sense of priority, my friend," I said, lifting his bag onto the bed, glad that I hadn't actually unpacked anything. I pulled that heavy leash out and clipped it to his harness. "Come on. Let's see if anyone out there needs help." I swung my bag over my shoulder and tucked the dog duffle under one arm.

The inner ceiling in the hall had collapsed a few yards toward the lobby, creating a pile of debris I decided not to bull my way through. Instead, Toby and I went the other way, toward the exit at the end of the wing. That let us out into the dog yard, which was one large pool of water, something that was only obvious in the darkness when I saw the reflection of lightning on the surface. We stayed on the sidewalk and made our way out into the parking lot.

There was no one out in the open when we stepped away from the building, and into the debris-strewn parking lot. The voices I'd heard before were silent. To say it was dark would be some kind of understatement. The sky above me was just black, lit only briefly by lightning that seemed to dart and flicker quickly across the sky. Looking around, I might as well have been in the middle of the desert, and not on the edge of a city. There were headlights on the highway, but no sign of artificial lighting anywhere else. Whatever other damage the storm had done, it had clearly taken down the power grid.

About then I noticed faint lights in the the hotel office, and from the way they moved, I assumed I was seeing flashlights. The office seemed the place to start, so we walked as quickly as we could across the parking lot.

Lightning continued to flash most frequently to the northeast, illuminating clouds from within, and low grumbles of thunder rolled across the land, but the wind had died and except for the sound of dripping water, all was dark and quiet in a surreal sort of way. It felt like waking up from a nightmare, only to find you were never asleep to begin with. Our path to the office was anything but straight, as we worked our way around the debris scattered across the pavement. The façade of the building was brick, and somehow undamaged, though the door was propped open at an odd angle.

Lights were aimed at me and at Toby as we entered the crowded lobby. I heard a voice say with evident relief, "There you are! Thank god, we're all accounted for now."

"Tornado?" I asked, wanting to be absolutely sure of what had just happened. They all stared at me. Feeling a little defensive, I shrugged and said, "I'm from California."

"Ah, right," said Mr. Willis. "Yes, a tornado. Looks like it just clipped us. Blew out windows, ripped off part of the roof, but no one seems to have been hurt."

"Just frightened half to death," said the woman with the shaggy dog in her arms. She no longer looked businesslike and seemed on the verge of tears; Kermie looked like a nervous wreck, and I felt nothing but sympathy for him.

"Me too," said young Kyle, who was up at adult level, held firmly by his father. His mother was standing so close to her husband that light couldn't have found its way between them. All three looked as if they'd taken a hike through a wind tunnel.

Emergency vehicles were screaming up the freeway frontage road. "Appears someone wasn't so lucky," muttered a man I hadn't met before.

We all walked outside to see where the first responders had gone. The flashing lights were already a long way off. "Is that a fire I see, off that way?" Kyle's father asked, waving a hand to the northeast.

"Damn it," said Mr. Willis, peering toward the pulsing orange glow, the only light visible. "Sure looks like one. That's all homes and shops over there."

"I wonder how bad it is," I said.

"We're on the west side of town," said Mr. Willis. "If that line kept on as the radar showed it on the evening news, the whole town got clobbered. Some places worse than others, I'll bet."

"Probably won't find out anything until morning," said Kyle's father. He nodded back toward the lobby. "So, what do we do now? Camp out in there?"

"Wait until Javier finishes checking the other wing," Mr. Willis said. "We had a few vacancies in there, and the storm seems to have missed it."

"Lucky us," someone in the crowd muttered.

"Actually," I said, "I do feel rather lucky."

"Amen, brother," said Mr. Willis, with complete sincerity. I could only nod in agreement.

A young Hispanic man in a T-shirt and jeans appeared, holding one of those flashlights that could double as a medieval weapon. He mercifully kept it aimed at the ground; the thing was incredibly bright. "Got a few shingles loose on the other side," he told Willis. "But everybody over there is okay, if a bit shook up." He glanced around at our group. "'Fraid we don't have enough vacancies for everyone, though."

"We could double up," said a young woman who had remained silent through it all. She looked at Kermie's owner, who was now carrying her dog slung over her shoulder. "You and me, maybe?"

We worked it out from there, with me ending up lodging with Kyle's family, partly at the boy's insistence. We finally introduced ourselves at that point. Kyle's father was Phil and his mother was Marsha. I made a token objection, offering to sleep in my SUV, and was quickly out-voted, four to one, with Toby's reaction to being reunited with young Kyle being the deciding vote. Truth be told, I was too tired and strung out by that point to argue. Kyle and Toby were firmly attached, by then, with Kyle clutching Toby's harness. Toby kept pressing his big block of a head against the boy's rib cage. The enthusiastic tail whip was back in full force.

We followed Javier around to the other side of the motel and he opened a double occupancy room with queen-sized beds. I dropped my bags in a corner and said I needed to retrieve a few things from my vehicle. Toby seemed reluctant to go back outside at that point, so I left him in the care of young Kyle, an arrangement that seemed to suit them both very well.

Outside, the clouds were breaking up. The moon was shining through wide gaps, high in the sky and almost at first quarter phase. It was a relief to have even that much light, even though it revealed a disaster in the parking lot. Trees had come down in several places, damaging or outright crushing cars. One compact car had been flipped over on its roof. I was at first relieved to see my SUV standing apparently unharmed in the parking lot, but closer inspection revealed that it hadn't come through entirely unscathed. There were some nasty-looking star-shaped chips in the windshield that would need attention. It was hard to tell for sure by moonlight, but the paint job on the driver's side looked worse for the wear. I decided to let these matters be problems for the next day. I unlocked the SUV and pulled my bedroll and a pad from the back. My roommates were accommodating people, but four people with two beds just didn't add up for me.

The storm, by then, had rolled so far off to the northeast that, although I could still see lightning flaring in the cloud tops, creating momentary glimpses of structure, there was no longer so much as a low rumble of thunder. Several more emergency vehicles roared up the highway, sirens unnaturally loud in the stillness. I wasted no time returning to the room.

We arranged things by flashlight, a process

that led to some awkward moments that we managed to turn into jokes. But when I said something about unrolling my bedroll beneath the window and leaving the family the use of both beds, the response I received was completely serious.

"Forget it, Paul," Phil said. "Maybe use the camping gear to make Toby comfortable, if you like, but take the bed. The three of us will bunk together on the other one. We were set on doing that when the storm hit. No way would Kyle have been comfortable sleeping on his own, and I doubt he's changed his mind about that quite yet."

"I'd argue," I replied, stifling a yawn. "But I am dog tired." Glancing at Toby, I added, "No offense."

Kyle found that amusing.

"It's settled, then," said Marsha.

Private needs were then handled by turns in the bathroom, and still by the irregular glow of flashlights. Toby was walked in the company of a small boy, which seemed to please both of them. I did, indeed, arrange a makeshift dog bed with the camping gear, and Toby sank into it, his toy resting between his forepaws. We all settled down, switched off flashlights, and tried to sleep.

« 8 »

I'd have slept longer than I did, but a hand on my shoulder brought me up to a room full of soft, pre-dawn light. Opening one eye, I saw Phil looking down at me with a grin. He raised a finger to his lips to keep me from speaking, and pointed to where Toby was snoring on the floor near the curtained window. And I do mean snoring. If he'd been sleeping when the tornado came, I might not have heard the thing in time. Marsha was seated on the end of their bed, wrapped in a brown bathrobe, rumpled and disheveled, recording what we saw on her cell phone.

*

"That's a silly exaggeration," said Sam.

"Yes, ma'am."

I grinned at her, which earned me a warm smile in return.

Aside from the staff, we were the only people left in the pet store by that time. Lacking anything better to do, three store employees had gathered to hear the tale I was spinning. Or wagging, as the case may be. One was the manager, so I was comfortable carrying on with the larger audience, assured no one would get into trouble. Now and then a phone would ring and someone would leave to answer it, always to return a few minutes later.

"You did seem to run into some good people, for the most part," she observed.

"That's not really so hard to believe," I said. "Contrary to popular opinion, I've found that the good ones are still in the majority."

*

Toby was not alone. Kyle was on the floor in the makeshift dog bed under a large bath towel — closest he could come to a blanket, I guess — his head resting on Toby's shoulder. They were both dead to the world, though how that boy could sleep next to the noise Toby was making remains a mystery to me to this day. His parents exchanged fond smiles, then grinned at me. Marsha pantomimed pictures going from her phone to me, and I nodded. I'd make sure I had permission first, but knew that was an image that would go over well on the Toby blog.

We kept it quiet, but the dog at least was soon aware that we were up and about. His stirring roused Kyle, who sat up with his eyes mostly closed, clearly not quite conscious. Toby solved that by sticking a wet dog nose into the boy's ear. Kyle's eyes popped wide open and a sound of disgust came out of him. Rubbing his sodden ear, he muttered, "That's gross!"

Toby just stood there, wagging that bullwhip of a tail around. Mrs. Vernon had said, during the chat at the Nelson place, that Toby loved children, and she clearly hadn't exaggerated.

Marsha disappeared into the bathroom and came out with the news that the power was back on. We took our turns freshening up and I packed the few things I'd taken out the night before.

"With the electricity back, maybe the café is open," Phil said.

"That would be welcome news," I replied. "Skipped dinner last night." Glancing down at Toby, I realized we both had. "Sorry, buddy. Ah, first things first, a walk and a bowl of kibble. I'll meet you over there, unless you catch up to me with bad news first."

A moment later I had Toby leashed, and together we went back to my SUV, where I stowed our things and scooped a generous helping of kibble into one of the super-sized steel dog bowls I'd been given. I filled the other with water from the big jug I carried in the

SUV. He ate and drank with great enthusiasm and efficiency. Not a morsel escaped. Looking across the parking lot as the kibble was crunched, I took note of the fact that the small diner, which Phil had called a café, appeared intact save for a couple of shattered windows on the side I could see. There were three people outside, cleaning up the mess, and a fellow I thought was Javier was taping big sheets of cardboard over the open windows. Phil and his family went in and did not immediately emerge, which I took as a good sign. My stomach was rumbling.

Toby did indeed need a walk. I cleaned up after him, and while I did so, heard loud slurping noises. He was drinking from a rain puddle a few feet from the dog area. "Hey!" I shouted. "I gave you clean water not five minutes ago. Stop that! It's disgusting!" He looked up at me, muddy water drooling from his muzzle, apparently puzzled by my concern. He shook his head vigorously, and it's a good thing I was in front of him, and not standing to one side. It would have been messy.

*

"Did he have any problems after drinking that crap?" Sam asked.

"Nope," I replied, shaking my head. "No ill effects at all. It was a recent puddle, after all."

"Still, you guys dodged a bullet there, I think," she said. "I've seen dogs get into bad

trouble that way."

"I don't doubt it," I replied. "And he did, once. That's how he came to be known to Dr. Nelson. You know, I never did find out what he ate that made him sick. Guess it doesn't matter now."

*

Back at the parking lot, I called my roadside assistance service about the damaged windshield. To my relief and surprise, they said someone could be there that morning, which I also took as a sign that the town had fared better than we'd all feared the night before. I put Toby in the SUV, made sure he had that toy, and rolled the windows down far enough to make sure cool air could get in. It was heavily overcast in any case, so heat wouldn't have been much of an issue, but I wasn't taking any chances. He protested loudly, as if he were being abandoned by his only friend in the world. I had to wrench myself away; it wasn't easy, and I didn't exactly feel good about doing it. When I got around to the front of the diner I found a covered patio and outdoor tables. At one of these sat Kyle and his folks; at another was the woman with the shaggy black dog named Kermie. She was dressed in sweat clothes and greeted me with a "good morning" and a weary smile; clearly I wasn't the only one short on sleep. I patted the dog, saying, "Hey, they really do let anyone eat here."

His owner laughed and pointed to the sign on the front door that read 'dog friendly.'

"I'll be right back," I said to them all, and jogged back to the SUV, where I liberated my passenger, leashed him, and trotted back, just in time to see a dark-haired young woman in jeans, T-shirt, and black apron, arrive at the family's table. She glanced my way, looked down at Toby, and smiled, clearly not intimidated by either his size or his breed. People at other tables were trying not to stare, and a few shook their heads in disapproval when I brought Toby in range of Kyle.

"We were waiting for you, before ordering," Phil said.

"Didn't need to do that," I said.

"Breakfast is on us," Marsha informed me, and waved aside any objection I might make before I said a word.

"Well, thank you kindly," I replied instead, and sat next to Kyle. Toby parked himself between our chairs, knowing which side of the table likely held the soft touches. And he proved quite correct, as a matter of fact. It seemed I was expected to order first, and I did so. The waitress took down everyone else's choices and said, "That's a handsome dog you have there, young fella."

"Oh, he's not mine," Kyle answered. "We're just friends."

"He's with me," I said. She patted Toby on the head and went back into the diner.

"Funny way to put it," Marsha said.

"Well, he isn't really my dog," I explained,

and gave them a nutshell account — sans law enforcement issues — of Toby the lost dog and my intention to see him safely home. To say they were impressed would be an understatement. I was asked how Toby had gotten lost, and explained that I really didn't know. Mercifully, that was good enough.

*

"They should have been impressed," Sam insisted. *"That was no small task you took on."*

Our small audience muttered agreements. A phone rang and we lost one briefly as it was answered. Then a couple of customers came in and I was down to an audience of one. Which was actually fine by me.

"It was no small dog, that's for sure," I replied with a laugh. *"But in all seriousness, Toby was a smart and extremely well-behaved passenger. Patient, too. He was no challenge at all to travel with. Mostly just napped on the back seat or sat up front with me watching the world go by."*

"I've been meaning to ask," she said carefully. *"You had him loose in the car?"*

I held my hands up defensively. "I heard all about that after the fact, believe me, from people on the weblog. I had no idea doggy car restraints even existed. And as it happened, we never had a hard stop along the way, much less an accident."

"Good thing, too," Sam said.
"Live and learn," I said. "Did a fair bit of that on this trip."

*

The food was pretty basic roadside diner breakfast fare, freshly prepared and in generous servings. I went for the eggs ranchero, and somehow missed that they were served on top of, not beside, the refried beans. But I was traveling solo, after all, and a dog who drank from mud puddles was not likely to be easily offended. So, with a shrug, I dug in. The food was quite good, and my appetite was unaffected by the previous night's events. My table mates ate with equal enthusiasm, and it was amazing to watch that small boy demolish pancakes the way he did. I found myself wondering who would win an eating contest, Kyle or Toby? Speaking of Toby, the diner's dog-friendly policy extended to a bowl of water and a couple of dog biscuits. Toby showed appropriate appreciation for the treats, which vanished, and the water, of which at least half ended up on my shoes. Fortunately, they were waterproofed.

"Toby," said I, "you are a slob."

That got a laugh from Kyle, a chuckle from his folks, and a puzzled look from a once again drippy dog. At least there was no mud this time.

As we ate, my phone buzzed; it was the

windshield repair service, on its way. I told them which vehicle to look for and said I was in plain sight at the diner if they needed me. Not long after, there was a truck parked by my SUV and a man working at the windshield. I was just finishing my meal when my phone rang again and my presence was requested. I went over and inspected the work while Toby inspected and approved of the worker, who was — no surprise — quite taken with Toby.

"He has such an earnest look to him," the man observed.

I signed off on the work and paid the bill. As the truck drove away, I inspected the driver's side of my vehicle. In the light of day it was easy to see where storm-driven debris had damaged the paint job. I glanced at the damaged vehicles nearby, still upside-down and tree-enshrouded respectively, and counted my blessings. Toby and I returned to our breakfast companions.

The lady with the small dog, who finally introduced herself as Beth, walked her pup over to us to renew his acquaintance of the Big Dog, and give proper and enthusiastic greeting to a Small Boy. Much licking, tail wagging, and giggling ensued. It was all such a delightful contrast to the night's misadventure. The waitress came out to warm up our coffee, and Marsha asked for news of the town's fate.

"Well, I haven't gotten a lot of news," the young woman replied. "I do know that nobody got killed, though there were some injuries. Twister sort of side-swiped this side of town and went on to mess up the fields out that way." She waved a hand in a generally northeast direction.

Javier was walking by with the last of the broken glass in a steel bucket, and paused. "Heard it was only an F2," he said. Then he rolled his eyes and shook his head. "Only!"

"Main thing is that it didn't go straight through town," said Phil. "I've seen that happen. It can be very bad."

"Count our blessings," said the waitress, moving off to the next table.

"I have been," I assured her.

"So," said Phil. "People are following this little road trip of yours online, you say?"

"They're following Toby, be be exact," I replied, taking a sip of coffee. "I'm just the last phase of his lost-dog adventure. His family set up the weblog in the faint hope that someone might do what I did, and rescue the big lug nut."

"Lug nut!" Kyle chortled around a mouthful of pancakes, even as he 'accidentally' lost track of a bit of sausage. The food never came close to hitting the ground.

"Let me have the address," Phil said, pulling his phone from where it was clipped to his belt. "We'd like to see how this all turns out."

I complied and he gave the blog a quick look, then smirked. "I'd say there are some real low-lives trolling this thing, but whoever is moderating the blog is more than their match."

"Teenage girl with more on the ball than

most adults I know," I said with a laugh. "Computers and graphic design are her thing, but she's got a way with words as well. She built that blog from scratch."

"Sounds like she should be on your payroll, someday," Marsha said.

They'd somehow missed the point about me selling out my share of the company, but I let it pass. "You know, she might well be, when all is said and done." I meant that, too. If she continued to develop her skills through college the way she had pretty much on her own, I'd be more than happy to provide a reference and point her to the right connections. I knew people in the business from coast to coast. "I'll have a better sense for that when we finally meet."

"Well," said Phil, "we are now following it. And later today I'll post a brief bit about our chance encounter with the intrepid travelers."

"Look forward to reading it," I said.

"Okay, so you don't like it," I heard Beth say. Looking over, I saw her lifting a plate away from a befuddled dog. Noting my regard, she grinned and said, "Our vet is always warning us about giving him too much people food. This little boy is such a fussy eater, that hasn't really been a challenge." She nodded toward Toby. "What about him?"

"Pretty sure he'll eat just about anything," I replied. I handed her the shallow bowl the dog treats had come in, and she scrapped leftovers into it.

"It's good food, but the portions are over-generous for me," she explained. "Well, he likes his cheese omelet and refritos, that's for sure."

Beans...

It was too late. The bowl was already polished and the dog was happy.

"I think that's probably enough treats for this guy," I announced, closing the barn door after the dog who ate like a horse was already out. "And we need to hit the road."

Farewells and well wishes were exchanged — this took a while between Toby and Kyle — and we headed back out on the open road.

Some hours later, Toby gave a whine of complaint. With a sigh, I rolled down a couple of windows a bit. Toby whined again.

"What are you complaining about?" I demanded of the dog beside me, who clearly fancied himself my copilot. "That was probably you!"

« 9 »

*

"So, you've learned a thing or two, now, about feeding dogs?" Sam asked, not quite suppressing her mirth. The pair of store employees who had returned laughed outright.

"Well, there's one thing I certainly won't feed a dog ever again."

"People sometimes get dogs into trouble feeding them leftovers," said the girl who had started out at the cash register.

"Well, Toby came to no harm, but that night I spent time online giving myself a refresher course on the care and feeding of canines." I shrugged. "As it happens, we never shared a meal with anyone else along the way, so I had complete control over what Toby ate.

He didn't seem to mind, so long as he ate."

*

That next day's travel was blessedly uneventful. We made it to Oklahoma City in good time, and although I was eager to see Toby back where he belonged, I'd slept poorly enough the night before that even with a stop for coffee along the way, I was done driving. We landed in the first hotel that came up on the phone as being dog friendly, and had a vacancy. I tended to Toby's needs, locked him in the room with his dinner, and went across the parking lot to yet another roadside diner to obtain mine. It was a good, quiet meal, savored in a leisurely way as the world outside gradually darkened. The waitress flirted with me. Come to think of it, so did the manager; I think he had some sort of contest going on with her. I laughed them both off, left a generous tip, and went back to the room.

I'd wisely opted for double occupancy. Toby was sprawled on one of the beds, sound asleep. I was reasonably sure the Vernons would have run him off the furniture, but I couldn't see any point to it. Once he was home he would surely resume his normal habits. He was snoring like a badly out of tune diesel motor when I came out of the shower. Groaned when I patted him, snuffled, and started snoring again.

Online, I logged onto the blog and found

that Phil had been true to his word. The story of the dark and stormy night was there, and drawing a lot of commentary, most of it, mercifully, of the OMG sort, and nothing abusive. Kyle weighed in and said he missed Toby, which endeared the boy to the Vernons. The picture they posted of Kyle and Toby snoozing together didn't hurt; it went viral as a matter of fact. When it was discovered that his family lived in east St. Louis, barely two hours away, the Vernons suggested a visit. Seriously. These people knew each other from a couple of blog comments, and were talking about getting the kid back together with his recently met canine friend. Of course, I did vouch for them, and the younger Vernons in particular took an immediate liking to Kyle just from how he described meeting Toby. The general tone of the blog comments shifted from dominance by "experts" who were convinced I would turn out to be some sort of dog-napper to variations on a theme of "oh how cute."

The general opinion was expressed that Kyle needed a dog of his own.

*

"Do you know if they followed through?" Sam asked.

"As a matter of fact, I do," I said. *"And yes, they did. As a result of that visit, which happened a couple of weeks after I left Toby with the Vernons, it was decided the boy really*

did need a dog of his own. Last I heard, Kyle and his folks were raising a golden retriever puppy."

"Excellent!"

"It was inevitable," I replied.

The big dog in the cage sat patiently, watching me as if he understood every word. The cat in the cage next door appeared to have died of boredom.

*

I managed to sleep pretty well that night, even with a sixteen-wheeler idling away on the next bed. That probably isn't entirely surprising, given the events of the night before. Up early the next morning, walked the dog, fed the dog, and this time left him in the room to get my own breakfast. He looked a little disappointed, and peered out through the gap in the curtains, clearly trying to guilt-trip me, but he looked quite relaxed when I returned. I had bacon and biscuits for him, so whatever resentment he may have harbored was very quickly forgotten.

As Toby munched on his treats, I checked the claw marks on his hip and had a look at that inflamed eye. The welts were pretty much healed, and Frank's treatment of that reddened eye was clearly working, as it looked well on its way to normal. He still looked like he needed to regain a few pounds, but was clearly recovering from his ordeal in the wilderness.

We headed northeast, switching to I-44, and were making pretty good time when things became a little — odd. Just before we came to Tulsa my phone, safely mounted to the dash, went off. It didn't ring, it emitted that ghastly emergency services squeal that no mere mortal can possibly ignore. Toby didn't ignore it; his protest of "ah-roo-oo" was almost as loud.

"Easy does it, buddy," I said. We were sharing the front seat and I gave his shoulder a solid thump. Then I tapped my phone to see what was going on, half expecting it to be a test. But it was no test. It was an Amber Alert. "God," I whispered. "Hate to see those, Toby. Means someone's kid is in trouble."

The terse text message gave the girl's age — all of thirteen years — and the description of the vehicle, a dark blue sedan, which had last been seen traveling north from Fayetteville. The incident was described as a 'stranger abduction.' I remember shaking my head as I dismissed the message from the phone. I'd just spent time, over the past few days, with some of the best people I'd ever met. The contrast between the feelings I'd enjoyed with the Nelsons and later with Kyle and his folks, and the thought of a child in such dire straits, was stark. It made me want to hit someone.

We pressed on and passed through Tulsa, where I picked up some snacks with the thought of avoiding a lengthy lunch stop. The plan was to reach Springfield in Missouri and stop for the night. If it seems I was taking the trip in small doses, that was partially to accommodate the dog. I've said that Toby was a good passenger, but if I drove too many hours straight, he became restless. Sarah Vernon had already explained that this was normal for him on road trips. The Vernons stopped frequently to see things along the way, and Toby was apparently unaccustomed to long, uninterrupted rides. So, I chose to be accommodating. It didn't feel like much of a sacrifice, and should only have added a day or so to the already leisurely pace I was setting.

By the time we reached Joplin, I was down to a third of a tank of fuel. When I'm on the road alone, it's my habit not to let the level drop much below that. It's a comfort zone thing. This time, it had consequences beyond anything I could have imagined.

10 »

It was just a gas station, two sets of pumps planted on stained concrete under dark green awnings, in front of a convenience store with a roof that matched the shades over the gas pumps. The windows of the store were plastered with advertising posters. Shady trees all around, with green corn fields on one side of the highway, a subdivision on the other. I've stopped at hundreds of such establishments over the course of my life and travels. So, it doesn't matter what the place was called or what side of the road it was on. Toby and I stopped there for a break and to buy some gas. Simple as that. People who know what happened read fate or God or some such into it. The way I see it, the dog needed to walk, the SUV needed fuel, and that's all there was to it. As a result, we were in the right place at the right time. That's how most unusual things happen, I suppose.

I pulled in behind a sedan parked at the pumps on the shady side of the concrete island, promised Toby a walk, and got out of the SUV. As I walked around behind my vehicle to get at the pump, a strange, uneasy feeling rose up in me. Something felt wrong. I looked around, but didn't see anything obviously amiss. As I took my wallet out of my pocket, the unoccupied dark blue sedan at the pump ahead of me registered. There was suddenly a cold knot in my gut. I went back to the driver's side of the SUV, pulled the phone out of its bracket and tapped it a couple of times.

Toby, no doubt sensitive to my body language, gave a concerned whine. "Hush, Toby. It's okay." You say things like that to dogs, even when you aren't sure it's true, and by then I was anything but sure.

This time it wasn't okay by a long shot. The vehicle in front of me was a match for the one described in the Amber Alert, make, model, and color. There'd been an update to the alert message; someone had gotten the plate number. That matched too.

"Oh, shit!" I whispered as I tapped out 911.

"911, what is your emergency?"

"This is in response to an Amber Alert," I replied. "I'm parked behind a dark blue Ford Escort, Missouri license plate." I read off the plate number and gave the operator the details on the location.

"Thank you. Units have been dispatched.

Please do not confront the driver. He is considered armed and dangerous."

We went back and forth about what I should or should not do, and I promised to call back if the vehicle moved. As the conversation ended, Toby suddenly went rigid, quivering, and bolted past me out of the front seat.

"Toby! Damn it..."

He didn't go very far. He scrambled across the concrete to the back of the Escort and stood there, growling and whining. After a moment he rose up to plant his forepaws on the bumper, staring as if trying to peer through the hood of the trunk. The whining became insistent, almost frantic. I glanced at the convenience mart and saw two men standing in the doorway, clearly having a less than friendly conversation. The shorter and heavier of the two had a shirt on with the same colors as those of the station — probably an employee. The taller, dark-haired man, who had his back to me, wore jeans and a short brown jacket. My heart was in my throat. There were no other vehicles parked nearby, so the man in the jacket had to be the driver of the Escort. Toby's attention being so firmly fixed on that trunk could only mean one thing. What to do? Haul Toby in and let the cops eventually handle the matter? Hope they could do so in time?

Toby jumped up on the hood of the trunk, surprisingly nimble for a big dog. His gaze was fixed on the shiny blue surface beneath his feet. He looked briefly my way, quivering and whining, clearly baffled the human wasn't doing what needed to be done.

The amount of adrenalin in my blood by then must have been nearly toxic. My lungs felt shallow and my heart was racing. I wanted to be anywhere but there, in that place and time. I couldn't just stand there and watch that vehicle drive away, but intervention on my part would likely have — consequences. Then I thought of the consequences the kid I was sure was locked in that trunk surely faced, or had already endured. But — armed and dangerous? Just what the hell was I going to do that didn't involve getting shot?

Toby stared at me and whined frantically. I was the human. I was supposed to fix this. And a sudden calm settled over me like nothing I've ever experienced. There were no doubts left, and that car wasn't going anywhere before the cops got there.

"Jesus, can you believe this place?" The otherwise unremarkable looking fellow in the jacket and jeans spoke as he neared the gas pumps. He was shaking his head and scowling. The other guy, still in the entrance to the store, was staring daggers at him, hands on hips. "Can't take any credit cards today, he says! Damn, and I'm running on fumes. And — hey, what the hell's with that dog?" He stopped dead in his tracks, staring.

"I'm not sure," I replied, feigning puzzlement. "Sorry about that. I'll get him down."

"Big sonofabitch," he said. "Hey, I don't suppose you could spare me a few bucks?"

"All I have is a card," I replied. "So I'm out of luck, myself."

He took a step toward his car, then thought better of it and edged around Toby, who looked up from the trunk and sort of leaned toward him. Toby growled, and glared at the man in a way that turned my blood to ice water. Toby hadn't looked that hostile toward the bear. With the bear, he simply stood his ground. If I was any judge of canine body language at all, Toby was gathering himself for a leap.

"Get that damned dog off my car right now!"

"Sure," I said. I heard sirens not too far off, but had no way of knowing if they were meant for us. My gut feeling was screaming that I didn't dare wait to find out. I stepped around as if to get at Toby. We were both within a couple of feet of the car and each other and I wondered if I could take this guy down before he pulled whatever weapon he carried. Heart hammering, I reached out to the dog as if to haul him off the car, while the man kept his eyes on Toby.

Before I could do anything of the sort, something thumped the inside of the trunk and there was a muffled cry. Purely by reflex I looked at the trunk, then at the kidnapper. He swore and reached under the jacket he wore. I caught a glimpse of his hand on the butt of a holstered pistol. In a heartbeat I realized I wouldn't be fast enough, but I turned on him anyway.

I wasn't fast enough, but Toby was. With a

feral snarl that raised the hair on the back of my neck, Toby jumped, cleared the gap between them, and hit the man chest-high with his full weight. The kidnapper went down with a shrill scream of pure terror, the dog squarely on top of him, the arm of the man's gun hand clamped tightly in those huge jaws. The sounds coming out of that dog as he shook the arm he held were nothing less than primeval. The kidnapper screamed again as Toby shook him so violently the man's head bounced against the concrete. He lost both the gun and bladder control. His eyes were bulging and white all the way around as I quickly stepped over and kicked his gun out of reach.

The shopkeeper was striding toward me with a heavy pry bar in one large hand. Seriously, he was the human equivalent of Toby, a man physically not to be trifled with. Behind him came an otherwise ordinary-looking woman dressed in the same company apparel, holding a shotgun ready.

"Hold up," I said. "He's..."

"Yah, we know," the big man said, not taking his eyes off the dog, who had the man's arm clenched in slavering jaws. The woman with him calmly aimed the shotgun at the kidnapper's head. "Wife spotted him when he drove in, remembered that alert thing. I was stallin' him about credit card problems. The cops are on the way."

"So, they already knew when I called?"

"More'n likely." He paused, looked at the snarling beast holding the whimpering kidnapper at bay, and said, "Good dog. Damned straight."

At that moment a pair of highway patrol cruisers, lights flashing but sirens now off, roared to hard stops on either side of the pump island, and an officer jumped from each, drawing sidearms as they did. Both were aiming at the man on the ground and the dog on top of him. One of them told the wielder of the shotgun to back off; she complied immediately.

"Toby!" I snapped. "Toby, come here!" And gave a silent prayer to things I'm not sure I believe in that he would actually obey.

He released the arm he held, snarling as if determined to get in a last word, then ignored me and trotted to the back of the blue Escort, watching the shopkeeper work at the latch. One cop rolled the kidnapper over and checked his pockets, producing a large knife and a ring of keys. He went to the sedan and waved off the crowbar-wielding citizen, both of them sparing Toby only a glance. The wife of the shopkeeper had vanished, then reappeared unarmed. Two more patrols rolled in, one of them a county sheriff's vehicle, the other from the highway patrol. Things began to blur together as the adrenalin faded. The officer with the keys checked them quickly, one by one; Toby watched the whole thing with keen interest, standing perfectly still. One of the newly arrived officers started asking me questions that I answered without thinking, even as I stepped forward and put my hand on Toby's harness, prepared to restrain him to the best of my ability. By then the kidnapper was wearing handcuffs, and whimpered something about being in agony.

The cop by the Escort found the right key and pushed the trunk up and open. He bent quickly, reached in, and lifted a slim body, bound hand and foot and loosely gagged, out of the trunk.

"Good god," I muttered.

The girl was wild-eyed and yelling her head off behind the gag. The female officer hurried to join her colleague as he sat the girl on the curb next to the pumps. They worked at the zip ties around her ankles and wrists, untying and removing the gag. It all went into a plastic bag held by the deputy. Toby stood just beyond all this, watching and whining, tail tucked between his hind legs. The officers were all keeping a wary eye on the big dog, though no one had yet admonished me to get him clear.

Toby tilted his head to one side and the girl made eye contact with him. One of the officers had just enough time to yell, "Hey!" as Toby plowed between them to get to her. Before the harness could be grabbed — the deputy was reaching for it — the girl threw her arms around Toby's neck and held on for dear life. In another moment she was crying like a lost soul, with Toby's chin hooked over her shoulder, just as he had done with Kyle the night of the storm. He sat before her and that rope of a tail raised dust from the pavement, it was sweeping back and forth so hard.

As the deputy took hold of the dog's harness, one of the highway patrol officers held up a hand to forestall him. "Leave be," she said. "It's cool. It's what she needs."

We all just stood there, amazed by what we'd witnessed, leaving the big dog to do whatever it was he was doing. The girl's sobbing gradually subsided to sniffles, her face pressed into his shoulder. An EMT vehicle roared into the parking lot. After receiving a nod from the female officer who seemed to have taken charge, I approached the dog and the girl. She looked up at me with shockingly red eyes in a pale face framed by dirty and disheveled blond hair, and whispered, "He was trying to get me out."

"He sure was."

"What's his name?"

"Toby," I replied. "His name is Toby, and he is a very good dog."

"Yes," she whispered. "Yes, he is."

« 11 »

Toby was at his obedient best when the paramedics approached. Both men patted him, agreed he was a good dog, and Toby was more than willing to stay to one side and let them get to work. Getting the girl to let go of Toby was another matter. The younger of the two crouched beside her and started by asking her name. There was a response, but I couldn't hear what she said. My attention was diverted at that point by the conversation between the sheriff's deputy and the other medic.

"Probably just a bone bruise," the older medic said. "Even if it's fractured, it's nothing serious. That jacket must have been heavy enough to prevent a bite wound."

"Or that dog knew what he was doing," said the female highway patrol officer, who now stood nearby. "Dog that size, that breed, I'm surprised he still has an arm, broken or not."

That all struck a chill of dread to my heart. I had no idea what the local laws said about a dog attacking a man, and could all too easily imagine this being a problem, even with these extenuating circumstances. I held my tongue, not wanting to draw attention to this potential issue by asking about it, and held tight to Toby's leash, which I'd finally had a chance to retrieve.

A truck from a local television station arrived on the scene as I helped the paramedics unhook the girl from Toby. The reporter, a young man in a suit that was clearly too warm for the weather — he looked more than a little heat-stressed — was herded away by two of the highway patrol officers. He made do with interviewing the shopkeeper and his wife. I couldn't hear what they were saying, but they sounded very enthusiastic. At one point I needed to move Toby farther away to let them work. The look on the kid's face just about broke me.

"Hey, don't worry," I said, crouching down beside Toby and looping my arm around his shoulders. "These guys need to check you out. Toby's just going to sit here and let them do their jobs." Red, swollen eyes peered back at me, but she gave me a tiny nod. "You guys are okay if he supervises, right?"

"No problem," the older of the two said. "So long as he doesn't start offering second opinions."

The younger medic kept up a one-sided

conversation with the girl, but got no other responses until he referred to Toby as her dog.

"He's not my dog," she said softly. "My dog is back home. She's probably really worried."

"Bet your parents are worried too," I said.

She nodded again, then said, "Polly will take care of them."

"Polly?"

"My dog."

"Ah, now that's a great name for a dog." To which she merely nodded.

"You'll see them all soon," the older medic assured her. "But we're going to take a ride in the ambulance first. Need to have a doctor check you over. We'll call your folks so they can come to take you home from there. That all sound okay?" There was nothing condescending about his tone. He just talked to her like he would have to any of us there.

She focused on him, thought for a moment, and then said, "Okay." Everything about her seemed emotionally flat, as if she were regarding us from a great distance. She looked at Toby. "Is he going to be okay?"

"I'll take good care of him," I told her. "And he'll look after me."

"He really is a good dog," she observed.

"Yes," I agreed. "That he is."

She stood up under her own power and started walking toward the ambulance, then turned suddenly to kneel by Toby and hug him. Toby responded by thoroughly licking her face. The medics got her back up and led her away. A moment later, lights started flashing and the vehicle roared off. The siren started when they reached the frontage road.

I found myself in a circle of law enforcement officers, giving them information on how to contact me. It was requested that I find some way to stay in town for a couple of days, long enough to appear in court if the judge so desired. I agreed to that, and seeing that the reporter was out of range, explained the nature of my mission.

"Wait, he isn't really your dog?" one cop asked. "Damn, he sure acts like you trained him yourself!"

"What he did today, that came from him, near as I can figure," I replied. "At least, nothing his owners have told me has hinted at special training that would explain what happened here."

"Big and smart," the female officer said. "Some dogs don't need much training. They just know stuff." She smiled and scratched Toby between the ears. "My kind of dog."

The reporter was edging toward us; the cameraman was already gathering footage. When the female officer intercepted them I said, "It's okay. I'll talk to them for a moment."

*

"I think I saw a version of that coverage," Sam said.

"The big cable news networks all ran that first bit," I replied. *"And then their own local*

affiliates started showing up at the hotel I picked. It was surreal. I managed to keep the Vernons out of it for a little while."

"They eventually got caught up in it, though, right?"

"They did, but it went okay in the end," I said. "And after the fact the Vernons reached out to the girl and her family. There was some human-interest stuff in the news about her being reunited with the dog who rescued her when they did. Didn't keep them in the spotlight long enough to do any harm, as far as I can tell."

*

We've all seen what can happen to folk who suddenly find themselves newsworthy, and I really had hoped to spare the Vernons that pressure. I led reporters to believe Toby was my dog, which wasn't all that hard, considering the bond between us he so openly displayed. I was damned if his real family was going to endure what I found waiting at the hotel when I got there, if I could help it. I was vague about his history as I fielded questions thrown at me as we went to our room, said he'd had no special training and had surprised the hell out of me, doing what he did. Which was true enough. Eventually enough other guests at the hotel complained about the chaos that quickly engulfed the hotel that management called the police. There were soon enough deputies and local PD officers on hand to damp things down until an actual news conference could be set up in the lobby. I could only hope the event would satisfy the media sufficiently to let me get some sleep.

And I needed sleep, or at least a chance to retreat somewhere out of sight. I kept getting the shakes as the image of that gun being drawn kept flashing through my memory. How close had I been to being shot, possibly killed? It wasn't an easy thing to think about, and I couldn't keep it out of my mind. But I needed to follow through on things I'd agreed to do, and so with Toby there beside me, I somehow managed.

I kept dancing around the edges of the truth, telling people I knew next to nothing about Toby's background — I really hadn't asked any questions of the Vernons about his training — said that we'd only just started traveling together, and that I'd rescued him in a campground. I told them about the night of the bear, which impressed the hell out of people as you might expect. I said I was on a road trip to clear my head and reassess my priorities in life, also quite true, and was damned glad I had the resources that allowed me to do so. They knew who I was, by then, and questions were asked about the business I'd left behind, so I plugged it and praised the new ownership arrangement. Toby sat through it all with the patience of a saint, and didn't so much as flinch when the bright lights came on. He looked around, sometimes panting, sometimes with that goofball grin his breed is known for. You'd have sworn he knew exactly what was going on and reveled in his celebrity status.

And people asked about his breed, in light of what had happened. I started by reiterating the belief on the part of Dr. Nelson that Toby was not pure pit bull, and then defended the breed when a woman categorized them as simply aggression waiting to happen.

"Well, if that sort of viciousness really was part of what these dogs are, just waiting to happen," I replied, "the police wouldn't have a suspect, would they? They'd probably have a corpse. Let's forget the stereotypes fed by people who would mishandle any sort of dog. The only dog I've ever been afraid of was a German shepherd that really needed to be on a sedative. Look at this guy here." I put my hand on his head and he looked up at me, tail wagging. "Toby showed his courage and his strength, but did so with restraint. He could have ripped that guy's throat out. Wouldn't have been a thing I could do to stop him. Instead, he just held the guy down and waited for the people around him to do what was needful."

"He broke the man's arm," said the woman with the clear breed prejudice.

"The arm of a man who abducted a teenage girl," I shot back. "Anyone really need me to spell out what he had in mind for her?" It was suddenly a quieter room, with only the soft sounds of people no longer comfortable where they sat. "And he was reaching for a handgun under his jacket, with the intention of threatening me, if he didn't actually shoot me. Color me *entirely* unsympathetic about his god-damned arm."

People actually applauded that.

*

"*I expect the authorities were unhappy with you stating his crime that baldly,*" *the store manager said.*

"*Uh, yes, I did hear about that,*" *I admitted.* "*They flew me back to Missouri to testify and the public defender gave it his best shot using my brief indiscretion, but it was almost all he had to work with. You see, the search warrant they served on the bastard's home turned up — photos. Of his other victims. He even kept records of where he buried their bodies, and those bodies had been recovered before the trial started.*"

Sam's eyes widened. "*I never heard about that! But then, come to think of it, there wasn't much coverage of his trial here in California at all. Oh...*" *It almost sounded like she was in pain.* "*Victims? More than one?*"

"*Three others,*" *I replied.* "*All in their early teens. Trust me, you don't want to know more than that. I had to — I endured the trial and saw it all. Still wakes me up at night. He copped an insanity plea, lost it, and was convicted on, well, I don't remember how many counts. Multiple consecutive life sentences."*

"Not the death penalty?" the manager asked. "He sure as hell deserved it."

"No, but then, that ended up a moot point. He was murdered by his cell mate."

Sam shuddered and sighed deeply. "What a world we live in."

"It has its darker moments, I'll grant you," I said. "But it's still worth living in. The other people I encountered on that trip are all the proof I need of that."

*

That night the local news was loaded with pictures of Toby, the girl — Alana — and the mug shot of her abductor. She was seen with her tearful parents as they thanked everyone who had helped. She said nothing at first from her hospital bed, and just sat there propped up on the pillows, looking hollow-eyed and utterly exhausted. Until at the very end when she suddenly said, loud and clear, "Thank you, Toby. I love you!" As far as I was concerned, that said it all, and I couldn't bring myself to watch any more of the endless talking heads' analysis and interviews with dog experts trying to explain how and why Toby had done what he had. They clearly didn't know any more than I did. I went online, wondering what and how much I needed to tell Toby's family. The decision had already been made for me. They'd been watching a news show and had seen us being interviewed, recognizing both of us in a heartbeat. They weren't the only ones; the blog had blown up. Sarah Vernon was losing her mind handling the rate of posting, but since it was overwhelmingly positive "hero dog" stuff, she was at least having fun. I told her to expect a call in a few minutes.

And a few minutes later, I was speaking not to Sarah, but to her father. "Hello, Paul," he said.

"Jim, I take it Sarah has filled you in?"

"Saw it on the news," he replied. "Damn it all, that poor child!"

"They tell me she's shaken up, but aside from some scrapes and bruises, unharmed," I told him. "Physically, at any rate. I don't even want to guess what it must be like inside her head tonight."

"Still makes me want to keep my girls locked up in the basement!"

"Has the feeding frenzy arrived?" I asked.

"The — what?"

"Media," I said. "Crowds of reporters."

"Not so far," Jim replied. "A lot of the blog followers twigged to it, but there's no contact information on the blog, now. No names. We even scrubbed Dr. Nelson's stuff off when you hit the road. It felt to me like an excess of caution, but Elaine insisted."

"Good call on her part," I said. "I've been spinning a yarn regarding how Toby and I came to be traveling together. They've bought it for the moment, but from what I've seen online just now, that won't hold up forever."

"Probably not," Jim said. He sighed audibly. "Not your fault, Paul. You and Toby did what needed doing. We'll handle what comes with all the grace we can muster."

"Pretty much all any of us can do," I said. "And speaking of doing what we can in the moment, I wasn't fibbing when I told those reporters I didn't know anything about what sort of training Toby's had. Seriously, fill me in. How the hell did he know to do that?"

"Short answer, I don't know," Jim replied, sounding helpless. "I can guess at some of it. His reaction to that young fellow, Kyle? Elaine is a pediatric physical therapist, and Toby is her assistant. He's been trained to be around and interact with children. That 'hugging' thing you described is something he was taught to do when a kid shows discomfort or distress. Toby is very good at it, and even the most fearful children fall for him quickly."

"You didn't put anything about that on the blog," I pointed out. "He's just described as a beloved family pet."

"Our regular vet advised against volunteering information that might make Toby seem — valuable. If you know what I mean."

"I do indeed. Loud and clear," I replied. "Amazing. What made you choose the big lug for a job like that?"

"We didn't, originally," Jim replied. "He was a house pet, plain and simple, with basic puppy and dog training that any responsible pet owner would use."

"That makes you one of a rare breed yourself," I observed.

"Don't I know it. Too many dog owners — well, never mind all that. When Toby was two years old Elaine ran into one of her patients one day, at the mall. Had Toby with her. He and that kid hit it off in a big way, Toby already being predisposed to like children, having been raised with ours. The way that kid fell in love with Toby on the spot gave Elaine an idea. She asked around, found someone with experience in the matter and, after that guy got over the shock of using a pittie mix for the job..."

"Mix? So, Dr. Nelson is right?"

"We got him from a shelter, nine months old, an abandoned pup. The poor guy. The kids fell in love at first sight, and Elaine and I weren't far behind. Our vet out here thinks he's got some Labrador retriever in there somewhere." I could almost hear Jim shrug when he paused. "So, not one hundred percent a dreaded pit bull no matter what you see at first glance. Not that we care, one way or another."

"Everyone he meets reacts to the obvious visual cues," I said. "Then he turns on the charm and that's that."

"He has quite the winning personality," Jim agreed. "So, his response to a distressed child, even one locked in a trunk out of sight, I can understand that. He's trained to respond to the sounds of a child in distress. Sometimes PT flat out hurts! He surely heard her in there, trying to call for help. But going after a man with a gun that way, that beats the hell out of me. Taking that bastard down — that must have been a response to what he saw as a threat aimed at you. How else do we explain it? Believe me, nothing like that has ever happened since he came to live with us."

"A dog of unexpected talents," I said.

"Seems like."

I explained that this situation was going to slow me down, since local law enforcement wanted statements and such. Jim allowed as how that was only to be expected. We said good night.

Turning to Toby, who sat with his usual quiet patience by my chair, I put my hand on his head and said, "Hero dog indeed."

« 12 »

The next morning started with a visit that gave me, briefly, a very bad moment. There was a polite knock on the door and, looking through the spy hole, I saw a young man in a sheriff's deputy uniform waiting patiently on the other side.

I opened the door and said, "Good morning."

"Good morning, sir," he replied. "You're Paul Ford?"

"That's me."

Toby crowded me at the door and managed to push head and shoulders into view just as the deputy spoke again. "I've been sent to ask that you appear at the station at..." He took a step back. "Damn! He's a lot bigger in person than he looks on TV."

A canine whine of concern was emitted.

"It's okay, boy. You just startled him."

*

"I've always wondered why people do that," I said to Sam. "Including me. Talking to dogs as if they understand the words."

"How do you know they don't understand?" she asked. "After their own fashion."

"I suppose I don't, not really." I looked at the dog in the wire enclosure. "What do you think, big guy?" The reply came in the form of crowding forward, tail wagging, delighted by my attention. "Maybe you're right about that," I said to Sam.

*

"You okay with dogs?" I asked the deputy.

"Sure," he replied. "I mean, I'm not what you'd call a dog person, but dogs can be good people."

"Trust me, this one certainly is," I said. "So, what do you need me for downtown?"

"Well, mostly it's the dog who needs to come to the station."

That's when the jolt of adrenalin hit me. "Is this about him jumping that bastard and putting the bite on his arm?"

"Something like that," he said. Then, clearly reading the look on my face, he hastened to add, "He's not going to the pound or anything like that."

"That's good," I replied. Trying to stay ahead of the curve I volunteered that I'd gotten his vaccination records. I pointedly did not mention getting them from his real owners.

"Don't think we need those," the deputy said. "The report shows no broken skin, and what the medics thought might be a break was just a deep contusion. Oh, and he has a mild concussion."

"Then why do I need to take Toby down to the station?"

"They want to hang a medal on him," the deputy replied. He grinned when he saw my expression. "Hey, the dog's a hero, sir. The mayor will be there, among others. He's, ah, running for reelection, you see..."

"Aha, got it," I said, smiling as well, and vastly relieved. Seeing no harm in it, I asked, "Okay, when and where?"

I was given a time and directions and said we'd be there, and started rehearsing in my mind the ploys I'd used the night before to make it seem I was Toby's one and only person. What I didn't know at that moment was that the Vernons had already been outed. So, there was some confusion, and embarrassment on my part, when I continued to play dumb about why Toby was with me as things were set up for the mayor's photo op. Someone passed me a tablet computer with a news story on it showing me the Vernons standing in front of their house, all smiles. They were ever so proud of Toby, it said in the caption, and were looking forward to getting him home.

Turns out I, too, was a hero of sorts, for being the one getting him back where he belonged. After all, if I hadn't decided to take the trip, the fate of a young girl might have been altogether different. True as that was, the last thing I felt that morning was heroic.

"Huh," I said. And with a shrug admitted to the true nature of the trip, and why I'd handled things as I had so far. No one seemed to hold it against me. "So, this is going to be live, somewhere?"

"Cable news," an ever so professionally dressed woman in the group informed me. "One of my colleagues will be with them, covering the family's reactions."

"Well, then, let's give the big guy his medal," I said. "We're both more than ready to get back on the road." I said that with a smile, and everyone seemed to understand.

Toby, as he had the night before, handled the hustle and bustle with complete aplomb. He was properly introduced to the mayor, a tall, thin man in a dark blue suit who rather reminded me of Abraham Lincoln. He clearly understood how to approach a strange dog. Remarks were made on Toby's size and fine manners. I learned then that security camera material from the gas station had been released to the media and would be the follow-up material for the story.

"So, everyone will see what happened," I said at one point. "I'd have thought that stuff might have been considered evidence."

"Yes, well, it got out of our control before we could lock it up," said the highway patrol officer who had turned up for the proceedings. I recognized her as the officer who had been at the scene the day before.

"Oh, hell, the world needs to see good things on the news, now and then," the mayor replied. "I've seen the recording. The two of you made a good team."

"I'd have been screwed if Toby hadn't been there," I admitted. "I might even be dead."

"Certainly looked that way, from what I saw," said the Mayor with a knowing smile. He waved aside any further expressions of modesty on my part. "You and that girl both owe Toby, big time. That's one amazing dog. And he really wasn't trained for that sort of thing?"

"Nope."

"We have K-9 units that could do that, and they required extensive training," said the sheriff. "So, consider us all suitably impressed."

In due time it was done. Toby stood up as the mayor put the ribbon with a yellow medallion on it around Toby's neck. I have no idea where they came up with that so quickly. The hero dog wagged and licked the man's face rather sloppily, to the delight of all, including the mayor. Like I said, he was clearly a man who knew and appreciated dogs. Pictures were taken, interviews done, and the only awkward moment came when Toby needed to take a walk. Not realizing why we were wandering off, a reporter and her camera crew attached themselves to us. He decided to take a dump while they were filming.

"Probably gonna need to edit that," said the cameraman.

"Probably?" the reporter asked, one eyebrow raised.

A little past noon all was said and done, and we were back at the hotel. I had lunch sent up, including a few extras as a reward for my furry traveling companion, who was most appreciative, if a bit tired. When we had eaten and Toby had settled into a mercifully quiet nap, I gave the Vernons a call. Elaine answered.

"Hey, Elaine, it's Paul Ford."

"Hello, Paul," she said. "We thought we might be hearing from you soon."

"How are things at Toby's old homestead?"

Elaine laughed and said, "A little crazy for a while, I must admit. But it's settled down now. Jim was a little stressed, but the kids just ate it all up!"

"They were on television," I said. "That had to be quite the thrill."

"It certainly was, for them. I could have lived without it. Thanks for trying to keep it all off us, by the way. It was a lost cause, but the people who came here for the story were mostly pretty nice about it all. Especially the cable news folks." She laughed again and added, "I think Sarah developed an instant crush on one of the camera guys."

"Oh, dear," I said.

"And how's our big boy?"

"Dead to the world, at the moment," I replied. "Fortunately, he hasn't started snoring yet."

"He only does that at night," Elaine said. "It's why he sleeps downstairs." She paused, then said, "We saw that security camera material. Toby realizing there was a child in distress, in that car, that doesn't surprise me."

"Jim filled me in on Toby's career."

"But that leap at the kidnapper, and holding him down until the police took charge, my goodness! We have no idea where that came from."

"Jim thinks Toby was protecting me," I said. "The more I think about it, the more that feels like the right idea. How else do you explain it? He knew that guy was a threat to a member of his pack — namely me — and he did what any self-respecting wolf would do."

"Toby could have killed that man," she said softly. "He has the strength. He's big and he's powerful."

"He's also a very smart dog with a huge heart," I told her. "You know him better than I do, but what I saw, while amazing, after the fact doesn't really surprise me."

We chatted like that for a while, and I was assured at the end that, while the experience had been a little hectic, it had been a worthwhile adventure in the long run. I could well imagine. Getting out of school for the day to be on television had surely appealed to the Vernon kids.

I eventually saw the video loop from the

security camera. Toby looked wary as the kidnapper approached, but didn't leap until I made my ill-advised lunge at the man, and the gun emerged from the jacket. Had Toby seen the gun from where he stood on the trunk of that car? I could only assume that was the case, which begged the question of what Toby had thought was happening.

Shuddering at the sight of my own person probably about to be shot, I shut down the computer. As I've said, I'm not one to dwell on what might have been. That habit served me well that night.

« 13 »

*

"I saw that video," said the girl who had been at the cash register when I came in. *"Dude, that guy really would've shot you! I'd have been scared half to death!"*

"I was," I assured her.

Sam had taken hold of one of my hands again, and this time didn't let go right away. I hadn't realized until that moment that my hands were shaking.

*

I meant for us to be back on the road as early as possible the next morning. The restaurant attached to the hotel was not listed as pet friendly, but Toby got a pass — and treats — as one would expect for a celebrity. And as expected, everyone wanted to meet him and have their pictures taken with him. As tolerant as that dog was, I was strict to the point of bluntness regarding physical contact unless Toby initiated it. Which he did, anyway, with just about everyone. He was feeling loved, and was apparently possessed of a near infinite capacity to take it in. Rivaled only by his ability to consume bacon.

I made sure he was not given anything remotely resembling refritos.

All of the above was to be expected, I suppose. The thing I did not expect was who we met in the parking lot after I checked out. I'd just tossed Toby's bag into the SUV and made sure he hadn't dropped that ugly stuffed dog toy — still amazingly intact — when a voice hailed me from the entrance to the hotel lobby. It was the receptionist who had checked me out moments before, calling for me to wait up. There were three people with her: a man, a woman, and a child, all of them fair-haired. The man turned and said something to the receptionist, who went back inside. The trio approached, and hadn't come much closer when I recognized one of them.

"I'll be damned," I said. "Toby, I think you have one more meet and greet before we hit the road." When they came close enough I said, "Good morning, Alana," and because Toby was seconds away from pulling my arm out of the socket, staggered toward them and closed the gap between dog and girl. Toby's tail was doing its lethal weapon wag. Alana put her arms around his neck, pale and slim against his dark brown fur. Toby hooked his chin over her shoulder, and the rest of us just watched. Not a dry eye in the group, I assure you.

Her father regained enough composure to step forward and extend a hand. "Thank you," he said in a rough voice. "I don't know how to thank you enough!"

"Not me," I said, after clearing my throat. The handclasp was firm and included the man putting his free hand over mine. "Toby did the real work."

"I saw the tape," he said. "You weren't going to back down. That was obvious. Could have gotten yourself shot."

"Pretty sure that's what would have happened, if Toby hadn't done his thing."

"A remarkable animal," he said. "And as big as we expected." He managed a ragged laugh as he said that and released my hand. "Under any other circumstances, I wouldn't let my girl anywhere near such a brute. But..."

"He is not a brute!" Alana said sternly.

"Have to agree with her on that," I said. "You know, I'd have figured you for whisking her home, quick as possible."

"The doctors were being extremely careful," her mother replied. "They just discharged her this morning."

"She's okay?" I asked.

"Bruises and a few cuts," her mother said. "And a slightly sprained wrist."

"Could have been worse," I said quietly, coming that close to belaboring the obvious, and going no further. They knew what I meant. Quite likely, so did Alana.

By that point, the girl was having a deep discussion of some sort with Toby; they seemed to reach some sort of agreement that was never shared with the rest of us. This was followed by both parents patting him, praising him, and getting the cold, wet nose treatment. They had questions regarding Toby's family, few of which I could answer. In the end I suggested going to the weblog they had set up for Toby. "It's open to the public," I told them. "Post a comment to the most recent entry. I've been talking to them all the while, and they're delighted by what the big fellow did. Proud of him."

"They should be," said Alana's mother as the girl stood up. "And we'll check out the weblog."

"Absolutely," said her father.

We all shook hands again, Alana last of all. She didn't hesitate when I offered my hand, shook it firmly, then seemed slow to let go. Had the strangest look on her face.

"Are you okay?" I asked, at a loss for what else to say.

Alana shook her head, then met my eyes and said, "I will be," very quietly, but with clear determination. She let go of my hand, still with nothing resembling a smile on her face. "You're an okay dude, Mr. Ford," she said. "Anybody Toby loves this much would have to be."

As they walked away, I patted Toby on the

head and told him that was probably the finest compliment I'd ever received. "Come on," I said then, opening the passenger side door. "It's time to get you the rest of the way home."

« 14 »

*

"An amazing young lady," Sam observed.

"That was my impression," I said. *"In part, I think she still hadn't processed what had happened to her. Much less what almost happened. But I've heard from them since, in the form of a Christmas card with a letter and a photo in it this past winter. She looked happy enough, to judge from the smile she showed the camera. And according to the Vernons, she and Elizabeth Vernon, Sarah's younger sister, happen to be the same age. They're close friends now, and Alana is planning a long visit with the Vernons this summer. Everyone involved seems optimistic about how she's responding to the experience."*

"No lasting repercussions at all?"

"Oh, what happened left a mark," I replied. *"I'm told there have been nightmares. She's apparently profoundly claustrophobic now — wasn't before — and doesn't handle being surprised very well. There's almost certainly more to it than that, but it's all I know right now. Oh, she's also studying tae kwon do and advancing very quickly."*

To that last statement Sam merely nodded.

*

We ended up making one more overnight stay. I could technically have done the rest of that trip in one day, but all the excitement had left me unable to sleep well enough, the last couple of nights, and I found myself running up on my limits. We made it to St. Louis in the middle of the afternoon, and I just had to stop. I contacted the Vernons with a progress report and apologies for yet another delay, and was assured they would much rather I played it safe. So, one more dog-friendly hotel, where mercifully — and perhaps strangely — no one seemed to recognize us. I contacted the friends I meant to visit in Chicago, learned that they had been following recent events, and arranged for a moderately long visit. They were quite disappointed that I wouldn't still have Toby in my company.

The next morning there was one last phone call to the Vernons. It was Saturday, so there was no concern regarding who might or might not be home when the prodigal pup returned. I gave them an estimated time of arrival, packed up, ate breakfast, and hit the road yet again, eager to finally complete my errand.

Actually, eager isn't the right word at all. Anxious describes it better. As I drove, I imagined a hundred things that could go terribly and ironically wrong, now that I was so close to taking him home. The chances against any of them coming to pass were astronomically high, but then, what were the chances we'd have had the adventures we'd experienced thus far? It all gave me pause, and made me more than a little skittish. When we stopped to give Toby a break, I double-wrapped the lead around my wrist and checked that stout leather harness twice. The rest area where we stopped was deserted. The traffic on the highway was light. Even the weather seemed to have mellowed out for the event, with the gentlest of breezes pushing white fair-weather cumulus clouds under a high, blue sky. The countryside through which we drove was green with trees and fields, a beautiful land on a fine early summer day. There was nothing whatsoever to be worried about.

I didn't stop worrying until I left the freeway and entered Toby's home town, a small community not far south of Springfield. The one in Illinois, of course. The map on my phone was easy enough to follow, and we ended up where we needed to be without a single wrong turn. It was just after ten in the morning when

I slowly cruised down a street lined with modest houses and well-kept yards, checking addresses as I went until I found the one I wanted. There was no need to double-check the house number, not the way Toby went off. He'd gotten steadily more excited as we entered familiar territory, and when the house was in sight, he went crazy, scrambling from back seat to front.

"Ah-roo! Ah-rooo-oo! Ah-roooo!" Ending in a howl. I swear the experience left me with a degree of hearing loss. But I couldn't help grinning and then laughing as I patted the dog on the shoulder.

"That's right, Toby my lad!" I shouted over the baying. "That's home! Let 'em know we're coming! Hell, let 'em know we're here!" I laughed as that stout tail whacked the headrest, thinking the banging noise alone might bring them running.

I pulled into a driveway that already held a large van and smaller SUV, blue and gray, respectively. Outside my door was a green lawn bounded street-side by a low, split-rail fence and shaded by an enormous old oak. I had just a moment to take in that scene, and then Toby was standing on my lap with his front feet, a rather uncomfortable arrangement — for me, anyway.

*

"No, seriously, it hurt," I protested. "It was

a lot of dog on one sensitive spot. Stop laughing!"

"I can't help it," Sam pleaded, still giggling. The two employees still listening in laughed outright. Both were female, which just figures, I suppose. "I can picture the look on your face!"

Seeing no way to win that one, I went on.

*

In self-defense I threw open the door before I even shut down the engine. The Vernons were flying out of their front door and Toby vaulted from my lap to the thick, dandelion-sprinkled lawn beside the driveway. It took me a moment to catch my breath, as I tried to get out of the vehicle without staggering. I leaned on the open door and watched the happiest imaginable reunion. It didn't take long for immediate personal discomforts to be mostly forgotten.

The noise coming out of Toby was incredible, a mix of howls and shrill squeaks, punctuated by a sound I can't even describe. It must have been deafening for the people mobbing him. Every one of them was trying to get a grip on the dog, and he was trying to lick and jump on each one at the same time. It was a wild tangle of human limbs and a large, wriggling dog that had me grinning from ear to ear. I hadn't thought past the idea that there would be happiness upon our arrival. What I saw was off the chart mad joy. I've rarely felt better about anything I've done in my life, than I did in that moment.

I nodded to myself, thinking it was worth every mile, every bit of trouble and dime of expense. It took quite a while for the chaos to subside. Jim and Elaine stood up and left their kids in a pile with the dog, crossing the space between us in a few steps. Both were grinning and tearful at the same time. As they drew near I held out a hand, but Jim stepped past it and embraced me like a long-lost friend. Or a brother.

"Thank you," was all he said. He sounded like he didn't trust himself to say more.

"Yes," said Elaine, taking her turn to embrace me, and then kiss my cheek. She held onto my hands as she stepped back. "Thank you for making our family whole again."

"Most welcome," was all I could think to say.

A shout of laughter turned us around in time to see Toby racing around the front yard like a thing possessed. He sprinted to the tree, ran around it, then dashed to the fence. Turning abruptly, he took off like a shot across the yard and leaped through the open front door of the house. There was a lot of echoed barking for a moment, then he came racing back out into the yard, and the kids ran after him, shouting and laughing.

"That's quite possibly the most beautiful thing I've ever seen," I said.

"It's right up there," said Jim.

"Incoming!" Elaine shouted.

At the last moment I guessed where Toby was heading, and dodged out of the way. He bounded into the front of my SUV, scrabbled around, then leaped back out with the lumpy yellow dog toy clenched in his teeth. Without a second's hesitation, he trotted, head high and tail wagging, to the front door. He disappeared inside, and this time didn't come back out.

"Well," said Jim, laughing. "That's plain enough. Come on in, and welcome to our home."

So in we went. It was a pleasant split-level ranch-style house, clean and well kept, though obviously lived in. You can't raise that many kids, to say nothing of a big dog, in a place and not have it show. How that all showed made it feel like a home. We made our way into the family room and found Toby lounging in a giant-sized dog bed, tongue lolling out, eyes shining, every ounce of him looking like a dog right where he belonged. The dog toy was on the floor in front of the bed. Off to one side was an old plastic milk crate containing several other items meant for canine entertainment.

The kids quickly and noisily followed us in, and soon all the Vernons were around me. I lost track of how many times I was hugged. I've rarely felt such a sense of welcome. It was more like a favorite uncle had dropped by than a near total stranger. We had a quick early lunch of sandwiches and lemonade, after which I was given a tour of the back yard and garden. Everyone had a garden bed of their own, that of the youngest being filled primarily with radishes and marigolds. These people had serious green thumbs. I was impressed, being the sort of gardener who kills plastic plants. Another huge oak dominated the far quarter of the half-acre lot, and in its lower branches was an elaborate tree house, beneath which hung a rope swing. It reminded me strongly of my own boyhood home in northern California.

I was free and honest with my compliments. It was a settled, comfortable environment, and I was quickly just another part of it. I don't recall ever feeling like an outsider.

That afternoon, when I'd settled into their guest room and cleaned up, I was told that there was a coming-home party to be held that evening. Various aunts, uncles, cousins, and a grandparent were due to arrive. I quickly got the sense that this extended family held such gatherings any time they could come up with an excuse. I skipped the usual protests of it not being necessary, realizing this was really about them as much as it was a show of gratitude. Either way, it was necessary.

Toby fell into what must have been his normal at-home habits almost immediately, but never quite let me out of his sight. I started to realize at that point how much I was going to miss the big guy.

The potluck feast later that afternoon was loud, happy, and plentiful. I think I ate more food that evening than I'd consumed since Toby and I hit the road together. It certainly felt that way. Jim's elderly father provided adult refreshments, and let me tell you, that old man knew his beer. Also, a knowledgeable single malt drinker. As the long twilight of the Midwestern summer faded, the grownups sat with their backs to the collection of foldable tables at which we'd feasted, drinking what suited us, while a gaggle of children and a big dog raced around collecting fireflies and mosquito bites. Many of those gathered hadn't been following my trek with Toby online, especially the elders of the clan, so I spent the evening quietly recounting the adventures, large and small, we'd endured along the way.

"Oh, I thought you should know," said Elaine toward the end of the story. "Alana's folks called us to thank us for raising such a fine dog. They'll be coming to visit in a couple of weeks."

"I'm glad to hear that," I said. "They seemed like good people."

"That poor child," said a blue-haired aunt, frowning and shaking her head.

"She's a lucky one," granddad Vernon said. "Been following the news? That bastard who had her killed a couple others."

That was the first I'd heard of it. "God," I muttered when he shared the few details he'd picked up from the news that day. "That's the sort of thing that makes you sick."

"That overgrown puppy out there actually saved the girl's life," said granddad.

I raised the short tumbler of scotch that was in my hand and said, "Here's to Toby, the hero dog."

They all joined me in that toast, and no one was kidding.

« 15 »

I stayed the weekend, and on Monday morning prepared to move on. The Vernon kids had been held back from school for the day, so the entire household was on hand when we made our farewells.

"You'll come back, right?" asked young Billy. "Toby will miss you."

"As it happens, I've been given a standing invitation to do just that," I replied.

"That you have," said Elaine.

"You, sir, are always welcome in our home," Jim added.

"Thanks," I said. "I don't have the words to tell you how much that means to me. And I will be back, someday. You're all welcome to visit me, too, you know. Lots of things to show you in California."

"No doubt," Jim replied. "And we just

might do that, someday."

"I'm checking into school out there," said Sarah. "UCSF. I graduate next year."

"If you get in, let me know," I said. "Especially if you need part-time work. I can arrange that."

The goodbyes went on, with each member of the family having something to say, and a hug to deliver. Sarah surprised everyone, herself included, by kissing me. All the while Toby stood or sat, tail wagging ever more slowly. Somewhere in that doggy brain the reality of my departure was surely registering. With the last hug, I reached down to scratch the top of his head. Toby bolted, ran back into the house, and then raced back out, the lumpy yellow dog toy hanging from his mouth. He dropped it between us and sat back, whining, the tail wag decidedly tentative.

"Hey, buddy, this stays here with you," I said. I knelt and put my arms around the big lug, truly realizing only then how hard this was going to be for both of us. The wag became more vigorous, but as I stood up those big brown eyes held nothing but unhappiness. The entire dog seemed to droop, like a partially deflated balloon.

Elaine noticed this and crouched beside Toby, one arm around him. "It's okay, boy. You're home, and now Paul has to go home too."

Toby uttered a low "ah-rooo," that sounded more like a moan, and whined. I gave him one last pat on the head, got into the SUV and backed out of the driveway. The Vernons were shouting and waving. Toby stood there watching, a picture of woe.

For a moment, as I drove away, I had the terrible feeling Toby would come racing after me up the road. No idea what I'd have done, if that happened. I kept checking the rear-view mirror, just to make sure. But he knew where home was, and he knew he was there, where he belonged. I turned a corner and drove on, and realized I was holding the steering wheel so hard my knuckles had turned white.

"Come on, old man, lighten up!" I muttered aloud. I reached for the windshield wiper control to clear the windshield, which was getting blurry.

Except, it wasn't the windshield.

« 16 »

Sam wiped her eyes with a tissue. "That must have been so hard," she said after clearing her throat.

"It was. I was amazed to realize, driving off, how thoroughly I'd bonded with the dog in such a short time." I shrugged and added, "I mean, we only traveled together for a few days."

"A lot happened in that short time," Sam said, composure mostly restored. It had taken me driving halfway to Chicago, the day I left Toby behind, to recover that much.

"That's for damned sure." I shook my head and sighed. "When I got to Chicago and filled people in about the trip I'd just had, the prevailing opinion was that I obviously needed a dog in my life. Everyone seemed to know of one that needed a home. I waved them off. I still had a lot of traveling to do, or so I thought at the time. Funny thing, not long after heading north into Wisconsin and my next intended stop, the restlessness that had sent me out on the road was gone. I'd worn it out and was suddenly and acutely aware of how far I was from home. It was as if I'd remembered that I *had* a home, in fact, in spite of what had happened to send me out on the road. So, I headed back west by the quickest possible route, with only that promised stop in New Mexico to visit with the Nelsons."

"They must have been thrilled to hear your story," Sam said.

"They were. It's hard to miss when you have good material."

"Doesn't hurt that you tell a story well," she said. The two store employees nodded in vigorous agreement, then went off into the store.

"Thanks." The dog in the crate made eye contact again, and I started to form a relevant question about his manners and personality. But as I put the words together, the cat revived, stretched, and yawned. The dog turned from me and put his muzzle against the wires separating them. The cat mewed and tried to rub its face against the dog's nose. "What's with the cat?" I asked. "You'd swear they were best friends or something."

"Well, actually, they are," Sam replied. "They grew up together, starting as puppy and kitten. Their owner died of cancer a month or so ago. We've been trying to adopt them out together. A few people have been interested in Sylvester, but the big dude, Moe, has been a deal killer, so far."

"Moe," and I chuckled. "What kind of name is that for a dog?" She gave me a patient look. The two animals clearly wanted to be in the same cage. I sighed and shook my head. "Sylvester and Moe. Well, I wouldn't want to be the one to break up the band. Though I don't know the first damned thing about taking care of a cat."

"There's nothing to it," Sam replied. "Trust me. I've been fostering these two since they became homeless, and know them pretty well. Moe is a sweetheart and Sylvester is a bit of a prankster, but has a heart of gold." She almost sounded shy when she added, "I'd be happy to help you get up to speed with them, if you'd like."

"I could probably use the help," I admitted. "Starting with picking up what I need for these two."

"Then we should probably get to it," Sam said. "The store closes soon."

"Oh, so that's where everyone else went," I observed. "Coming up on that time."

There was paperwork to fill out, and a fee for the dog license. Both animals were up to date regarding vaccinations. We put Sylvester in a carrier, which he handled like a pro, then let Moe out and harnessed him. From the look I got from that dog it was plain as could be that he knew what was happening, and approved with all his doggy heart. I could already see that, much as he resembled Toby, he was his own style of dog, and that was fine by me. Sam tied the leash to the shopping cart we used, and I went on something of a spending spree, aided by Sam and the store manager, who seemed not at all perturbed that I was keeping him open past regular business hours. Halfway down the dog-toy aisle I stopped dead in my tracks, staring at a familiar, lumpy yellow dog toy.

"I'll be damned," I said, holding the thing up to her.

Sam was quick on the uptake. She just smiled and laughed as I tossed the toy into the cart.

I helped her pack up and load her car, then we exchanged contact information for the stated purpose of being in touch should I need advice or assistance. We turned out to be neighbors, indeed, living less than half a mile from each other on the same street.

"Could I talk you into dinner, sometime?" I asked.

"That sounds good," she replied. "I'm actually free tonight — oh, but you've got these two to settle in."

"Well, you did offer to help with that. Say, do you like pizza?" I asked. Then, having already spoken on impulse, I threw caution to the wind. If she took it the wrong way... "I know a good place. They, ah, deliver."

She gave me a quizzical look, but to my relief there was nothing of suspicion in it. Like I said at the beginning, we were neither of us children, though at that moment I felt a none too distant echo of my adolescent nervousness around pretty girls. Then a smile was there, and Sam nodded. "That sounds like a great idea. It will help introduce them to their new home if I'm there for a while." She gave me a wink and my heart skipped a beat.

So, she followed me home, and in the end it turned out to be a four-way rescue. Sam had a story of her own, and it wasn't an entirely happy one. But I listened, as she had listened, and between the two of us we found a way to make ourselves whole again, and then to share that wholeness. When the time came, we traveled east to see old friends, and Toby met Moe. It took all of a heartbeat or two for them to become friends, and everyone fell in love with Sam. The kids we've adopted and fostered since that trip, with four feet or two, have all done well, and if it hasn't always been 'happily ever after,' life being the chancy business it sometimes is, neither of us has any regrets. It's been good.

It still is.

About the author...

Thomas Watson is a writer and amateur astronomer in Tucson AZ. Generally a spinner of more fantastical tales, he is occasionally seized by the urge to write outside of the usual box. He always gives in to that urge, and this time it led to a tale of a tail wagging. He never knows where the stuff of daydreams will take him, but the trip is usually worth it. He also loathes writing about himself in the third person, even if it's considered "professional" in some circles. It sounds pretentious, and besides, it feels like walking backwards up a flight of stairs.